Things I Want You To Do

Stories

William Marquess

Fomite

Burlington, Vermont

ISBN-978-1-947917-45-3
Library of Congress Control Number: 2020934051
Fomite
58 Peru Street
Burlington, VT 05401
www.fomitepress.com

To Emily and Joel, again

"All that you've loved is all you own."
— Tom Waits, "Take It With Me"

With thanks, again, to my beloved family and friends,
and to Donna and Marc, editors extraordinaire.

Contents

Her Mother's House

The first surprise was her mother's death. No, the first surprise was her father's voice on her answering machine. It had been so long, she wondered for a moment why it sounded so familiar. She hadn't recognized the caller I.D., and didn't pick up. But then there it was, the raspy, prepossessing tone of Donald T. Simon himself. "Ruthie? Are you there? Pick up!" When was the last time they talked? Did he even know that Mac had left her five years ago? Six years. She kept forgetting it was 2019 now.

She picked up, and he gave her the second surprise. It was sudden. He didn't know much about the details. He and her mother had been separated for all these years. But when her heart failed, at seventy-eight—"God, how could we be seventy-eight?"—and her minister got in touch with him, he knew he had to be the one to let their daughter know.

Her minister? The mother Ruth knew had been thoroughly secular. And Jewish. Did he mean rabbi? She wasn't ready to ask. Then came the next surprise.

"Ruthie, we need you to write something."

"Write something?"

"Yes. You know, something to say at the service."

"The service?" She was stuck on Repeat.

"A week from Saturday. At her church. In Upper Montclair."

"But Dad—"

"You were always such a great writer. You know I can't do it, I never could write for shit." He laughed. "And this minister, I don't think she knew your mother at all. She says we need a voice from the family. Who else could it be? It has to be you."

Well, he was right about his own writing talents. And also about the lack of other candidates. Ruth was an only child. And her mother had been an only, too, so there weren't any siblings to call on. Ruth had always longed for an aunt. She thought Mac's life had been shaped completely by the presence of his older brother, who freed Mac to be the happy fuckup of the family.

But how could she write something? She hardly knew anything about her mother. They'd never been close. She never even *liked* her mother. What would she say?

"Ruthie?"

"Yes, Dad."

"Good. I knew you'd understand. You'll be great."

And so they made plans.

It wasn't fair to say she had never liked her mother. The woman had given birth to her, tended her in childhood—

with the help of nannies and maids—and always wished her well. Ruth couldn't quibble with that. But she had never quite *respected* Twyla Robinson Simon. She pictured her mother sitting at a vanity, daubing at her makeup in front of those bright little lights. Or at the wheel of the big Lincoln, waiting for Ruth to emerge from some kind of lesson—piano, dance, painting, there were always lessons. Her mother idled the engine in summer for the AC, in winter for the heat, even though she knew it drove her daughter crazy. Ruth grew up during the Arab oil embargo, with Jimmy Carter wearing cardigans in a chilly White House. Her fourth-grade teacher taped a little picture of the Earth above every light switch, with the caption "Love Your Mother! Turn Off The Light!" When her mother saw Ruth coming toward the car, she cut off the engine.

Ruth could not get out of suburban New Jersey fast enough. Off to college, off to Paris for study abroad, off to a teaching job in Vermont. Her first career goal was to be everything her mother was not. Her mother wore a chinchilla stole, preserved in its entirety so that when you fastened the clasp it was biting its own tail. Ruth had nightmares about those beady dead eyes. She became a professor of Environmental Studies in order to teach young people not to idle the engine. And now she was supposed to write something. Something respectful. A daughter's lament.

She did not plead with her father about her own bad health. She couldn't remember how much he knew. He must remember her diagnosis with breast cancer eight years ago. Nine. But maybe he thought that when she got through the first round of chemo and radiation, she was in the clear. Maybe he didn't know that she lived from scan to scan, and went back on chemo when things looked dodgy. It was like dating again—sporadic, uncertain, exhausting. How could he know? She hardly told anyone, except her eighteen-year-old daughter, Harper, who had moved back in recently. She was determined not to use it as an excuse. Her father didn't need to know.

When she googled her mother's name—knowing this was pathetic, but still—all that came up was a Facebook page for The Ladies Auxiliary at the Upper Montclair United Methodist Church. Shouldn't there be an apostrophe after "Ladies"? Who called themselves "ladies" anymore? And what was an auxiliary? The page was unforthcoming, but at their next meeting, it said, they would share memories of Twyla. This Sunday night. Ruth decided she had to be there. She would drive down and spend the week at the house where she grew up, help get it ready for the market. Her father was going to let the real estate people take care of it all. But shouldn't someone go through her mother's things?

By e-mail, she told her students to work on their projects in Burlington. Each of them had been assigned an environmental issue to study. February was a slow month in the classroom, anyway; it would be good for them to get out in the streets. She would take her laptop, and expect electronic reports. And of course, they should also follow the media, as always, for news about the welfare of the planet. This President seemed intent on dismantling all the meager progress made by the previous one. But it was never too late, she told them, until it was too late.

Harper wanted to join her in New Jersey — which was sweet, considering that her grandparents had ducked out of her life at the time of their divorce, when she was ten. She couldn't take a full week from her waitressing job, but Ruth offered to cover the airfare for the following weekend. She would stay with her grandfather in the city and drive with him to the service on Saturday.

Driving south in late February is time travel: the miles roll the season ahead. In northern Vermont, the pines were iced, the fields still deep in winter dreams. As the Subaru raced down the Taconic that Sunday afternoon, the snow cover thinned and crows collected in roadside oaks. Rolling down her window at an interchange near the city, Ruth thought she caught a whiff of something like Spring. Marsh grass quickening? Frogspawn? Maybe it was just a tang of thawing sewage.

And maybe she was being wishful. By the time she drove into Montclair, sleet was leaking from leaden clouds, ice piling up on her windshield faster than the wipers could scrape it away. The real estate agent had agreed to meet her at the office on a Sunday, just to give her a key. Ruth was late, as usual. One of her colleagues said that her tombstone would read "Here Lies the Late Ruth Simon." The realtor, a middle-aged woman in a sweater and jeans, asked her, "Do you think this winter will ever end?"

"Oh, I bet it will," said Ruth. She hated talking about the weather.

The woman cocked her head but didn't bite. "Well," she said, "we'll get the house ready for showing as soon as you've gone through it." She handed Ruth a stack of flat U-Haul boxes, a dispenser of packing tape, and a house key — probably the same key Ruth had once owned, back when she lived there with her parents. Ruth thanked her and hurried back into the sleet. At five o'clock, it was already dark.

The Twyla gathering of the Ladies Auxiliary was being held at a home not far from their old neighborhood. It was bound to be awful — but she had said by e-mail that she would go, and there was no ducking it now. She'd just pop in and say hello. Maybe they'd have something to eat.

The GPS took her to one of the newer developments, where massive McMansions loomed on knolls among trees that protected them from contact with the neighbors. It was too dark to appreciate the many architectural styles, but it was a land of lovely lampposts. Her destination was a gravel parking area full of Navigators and Escalades. A sandstone path led from it toward a hulking house, crossing an ornamental pond along the way. It was illuminated by lights in the water, from which rose tendrils of steam. As Ruth hurried across the bridge, a huge golden creature darted through the water toward her. Well, of course: it was a koi pond. She was so startled that she slipped on a patch of black ice and fell, scraping her knee under her jeans. But she got up and soldiered on.

The house was a Spanish hacienda, a confection of stucco and red roof tiles. She was welcomed warmly by the hostess, a tall woman somewhere north of seventy, with a leathery complexion and a billowing crimson caftan. Her name was Taffy. She took Ruth's big dun-colored down coat and asked her to leave her wet boots in a heavy plastic tray. On a table in the entrance hall was an eight-by-ten photo of the President, signed with an illegible flourish. They took a step down to a vast sunken living room, where ceramic table lamps made pools of light far below the beams of a cathedral ceiling. The dark hardwood floor was softened by Persian area rugs and runners, any one of which would have cost more than all the furnishings in Ruth's little living room. Jazz piano tinkled from an unseen speaker, and the furnace was set at least five degrees too high.

"It's Ruthie!" someone cried. "The famous daughter!"

Taffy introduced her to five or six women of a similar age and appearance — velvety fabrics, curated tans, gouts of silver and gold at necks and ears and wrists. Ruth's hand went to her own pale throat; she couldn't remember the last time she had worn a necklace. There was a Donna, a Beth, a Luann; Ruth didn't get them all. They apologized for Frieda and Sukie, two of the "Auxes" who were still in Florida. But they'd be back for the service, someone said. They wouldn't miss it.

"Red or white?" said Taffy.

"Excuse me?" said Ruth.

"Wine," said Taffy, gesturing at a table that bristled with bottles. "Red or white?"

"Um, red," said Ruth, who usually didn't drink.

The women huddled about her on one of the Persian carpets. Donna, or maybe Luann, offered her a tray of skewered items, all of which included meat. Ruth, a vegetarian, took one and held onto it until she could deposit it discreetly on someone's discarded plate. A bead of sweat gathered at her temple, and her injured knee was throbbing. She sat on a sofa as big as a schooner.

These women seemed to know everything about her. Someone asked how Harper was doing. Was she still taking classes at the community college? Someone asked about Ruth's teaching. It must be hard to take this time from her busy schedule. Someone mentioned Mac, and all the ladies pursed their mouths in unison. Ruth hardly had to speak.

"But tell us about your mother!" someone said. "You must have so much to say."

Ruth cleared her throat, but nothing came out. "Moon River" purled in the background.

"Well," said Taffy, "You must still be in shock, poor thing."

"Your mother was such a great lady," said someone.

"She was so glamorous," said someone else. Everyone nodded. "She had such a sense of style."

She did? Ruth had always thought that she had got the worst of her parents' physical traits—her mother's squat body, her father's frizzy hair and beaky nose. In junior high she had starved herself to be more svelte, unsuccessfully, and started wearing her glasses low on her nose, hoping to flatten that owlish curve. There they perched still.

"Your mother," said one of the women—Luann?—"was my go-to for weather reports. She always had the Weather Channel on." Everybody nodded. "I used to call her whenever I needed an update. I could have looked it up myself, but it was more fun consulting Twyla."

Ruth nodded and smiled.

"She was such a gifted artist," said another woman. "I love her watercolors."

Watercolors? This must have been a recent pastime.

"She was so spiritual," said another woman, and everybody nodded. "Nobody knew her God better than Twyla."

Taffy poured a second glass of wine, and Ruth got a little drunk. They thanked her for coming; she thanked them back. Someone thanked her for everything she did. She wasn't sure what that meant, but she said, "No, thank *you*." Then she said she needed to be going; it had been a long day.

"Oh, of course, honey!" Taffy got her coat. They all said they would see her on Saturday.

Slightly tipsy now, she drove through her old home town. Past the school, the Presbyterian church, the culvert where she fooled around with Johnny Torrens. Past the cute little commercial strip, with its post office and drugstore. Past the country club where she spent long, boring summer afternoons by the pool while her parents played golf. Here was their quiet cul de sac. And here was the shadowy outline of their old house, two stories of mustard-colored masonry. In the dim streetlight she saw that it was still covered in ivy. Every year her father said they ought to tear it out, because it damaged the façade and would eventually pull down the gutters. And every year her mother said that bit of greenery gave the house its charm. As usual, they were both right.

By the time she unlocked the front door, she seriously needed to pee. She rushed in and found that the downstairs half-bath, which her mother called "the powder room," was locked. Ruth had always liked that bathroom, with its cushioned settee and its afternoon sunlight, muted by the wavy window glass. The master key didn't fit. So she had to tramp upstairs, still in her wet boots. At least the upstairs bathroom was standing open.

It was cold and awkward, sitting on the toilet in her coat and scarf, but it was thoroughly familiar. Immediately to her right was the bathtub, with the shower curtain featuring a naked water nymph, rosily curvaceous in the early *Playboy* style. Ruth remembered herself as a stumpy eight-year-old, staring at that creature as if it was a different species. And she remembered sitting here, on the closed lid, as her mother took her nightly bath. She always wanted company, and her husband was not going to sit on the toilet to chat while she shaved her legs. On the high windowsill, a transistor radio played the hits of the day — The Carpenters, The Captain and Tennille. She smoked a single Lucky Strike, ashing it in a tray at the edge of the tub. She said it was how she timed her soak. The smoke mingled with the steam, obscuring the black diamonds on the white tile walls. Tonight, there was no whiff of tobacco; her mother had quit smoking long ago.

Apart from that bit about timing the soak, Ruth could not recall a word from all those bath-time chats. She remembered the steam, and her mother's nakedness — the soft, full breasts, the startling black patch of pubic hair. She remembered the disc jockey's name, and every word of "Love Will Keep Us Together." But what did her mother say?

On the phone, her father had told her not to bother with any cleaning. The real estate people would bring in professionals, he said. "Just take what you want, and the rest can go in the estate sale. You know that place is going to be overflowing with junk she couldn't bear to throw away." He laughed. "After we had lived there a few years, I stopped going into the basement. Just setting foot down there was an invitation to a sprained ankle."

Ruth took off her boots and set them in the bathtub. She couldn't bear tracking more sludgy water around the hardwood floors. She stepped into the master bedroom, where she found the bed unmade and the furniture in disarray — night table and bedside chair pushed out of the way, hard against the vanity, its stool overturned. She set it back on its legs. In the closet, she discovered a pair of red cloth slippers, a little large, but close enough. They made a soft *shuss-shuss* as she went downstairs. She took a roll of paper towels from the kitchen and set herself to cleaning her tracks from the front hall, the stairs, the upstairs landing, the bathroom. In the soft light of the hallway sconces, the old wood regained its sheen.

She shussed back to the kitchen, and blinked in the yellow glow. Her mother had said that a kitchen should always be yellow. Ruth doused the overhead light and went to the stove, where she flipped the toggle switch on the exhaust hood. Her mother liked to leave this light on at all times, a night light for the whole downstairs. When Ruth was in her teens, she switched it off every time she walked through.

The fridge and pantry were brimful of stuff. Ruth thought she recognized some spice jars from 1988. The electric kettle was half full. She boiled the water and tore into a cardboard cup of ramen that looked safe. Then she sat at the old breakfast table in the soft stove light. Best meal she had all day.

And then she shussed around the house. It was, as her father had predicted, a mess. Not that her mother had been a poor housekeeper. She had always employed a cleaning woman, and it was clear that someone had dusted not long ago. But a cleaning woman could do only so much about the proliferation of stuff that cluttered every surface of every room. Tchotchkes and stacks of magazines, candlesticks and salt cellars, coasters and napkin rings. On the living room coffee table there was a collection of driftwood that looked like a workshop for antler sculptures. It was all so familiar—and all so strange. Ruth had lived here for eighteen years, but now, in another century, she felt like a tourist, uncertain of the local dialect. Her father was right: she should let the professionals take care of it.

In the den there was a hutch full of bric-a-brac, with a shelf of photos preserved in plastic holders. Here was baby Twyla in black and white, in her mother's arms. Here was a high school portrait, Twyla in pink chiffon. And here she was at the beach, looking on as little Ruthie worked on a huge sand castle. Twyla beamed. She was so young.

On a lower shelf, Ruth found an old Magic 8-Ball. She remembered when her mother showed her how to use it, back when she was twelve or thirteen. "You see the window here? That's where you get your magic answers. First, you hold the ball window-side down, like this, and you ask it a yes-or-no question."

"Like what?" Ruth said.

"Oh, like 'Is it going to rain today?' Then you turn the ball over, and you'll see the magic answer float to the surface in the window." Her mother turned the ball, and the two of them watched as a blue triangle with white words on it drifted into view. "See? It says 'Most Likely.'" Her mother pointed at the rain outside, and laughed. "I told you it was magic."

Ruth said, "That was too easy. It's always raining here."

"All right," said her mother. "I'll do another." She held the ball at her chest, window side down. 'Am I not beautiful?'" she asked, in a fluting voice. Then she turned it up again, and cried, "Ha!" Ruth peered over her shoulder. The ball said, "It is decidedly so." Her mother said, "You can't get more beautiful than that."

Ruth said, "That thing is rigged," and left her mother to this frivolous pastime. But later that evening, when her parents were chatting in the living room, in their usual chairs, she slipped into the den and tried her own interrogation of the ball, all in a whisper.

"Will I pass Algebra?" she asked.

"Ask again later," the ball replied.

Well, there was nothing magic about that. She thought for a moment, then asked, "Does Johnny Torrens like me?"

"Don't count on it," said the ball.

She nodded. Just what she thought. Then she tried again. "Will I keep all my teeth?" Ruth had a thing about her teeth.

The ball said, "As I see it, yes."

OK, that was better. She paused. Might as well go for a big one. "Will I be happy?" she whispered.

The ball said, "Better not tell you now."

She threw the thing into an overstuffed chair. Stupid toy.

Now, as she stood in that same room, there were so many questions she wanted to ask. Will I live out the year? Will Harper be OK? Can I be a better person? And she couldn't stop the questions from pivoting into the past tense. Did I drive Mac away? Did I fail my mother?

She set the ball back on the shelf. Better not to know.

Then she went upstairs and checked the bed in her old room. The sheets seemed clean, as if no one had slept there in thirty years. On a bookshelf crowded with self-help books and cute ceramic angels, she found an old copy of *Alice's Adventures in Wonderland* and *Through the Looking-Glass*. Inside the cover was an inscription in her mother's upright hand: "To Ruthie, from The Queen of Hearts." Did her mother not know that the Queen of Hearts was an ogre?

She was exhausted. Decisions could wait for tomorrow. She brushed her teeth, stripped to her underwear, and climbed into her old bed.

But sleep did not come. She was too tired, and the air in that room was too dense. The white glow of a streetlight slanted through the blinds, and the furnace kept kicking on and off, trying too hard, as it had always done. After about an hour, she got up, put on the slippers, and shussed down the hall.

Between her room and her parents'—she should say her mother's, as her father had not lived here in years—was a large walk-in closet. It smelled of camphor, as it always had. On a high shelf, Ruth found just what she was looking for—a sleeping bag and a foam rubber pad to go under it. She cleared some space on the closet floor, snugged the pad into a corner, and unrolled the sleeping bag on top. Then she closed the door, turned out the light, and crawled into the bag.

At age ten, this closet was her haven. She had slept in here off and on, in this very sleeping bag. Her father never knew; he would surely not have approved. But her mother must have seen the bedding, must have noticed that Ruth was not in her own bed. And she never said a thing.

Now, as then, it was intensely dark and quiet. No furnace, no street light, none of the voices of the house, the echoes of things not said. On this night, in her haven, in her mother's house, Ruth was asleep in minutes.

In the morning, she tried her laptop at the kitchen table — and got nothing. Trying to reboot, she discovered that the battery was kaput. And then she found that she had neglected to bring the charger. Any writing in this house would have to be done by hand. Her phone was similarly blank: no reception. But when she tried the landline on the kitchen wall, she found the old reassuring dial tone.

She walked to the convenience store half a mile away. It was a wan and chilly late-winter day; discarded cups and cans peppered the scurf of old snow along the sidewalk. Ruth was always disgusted by the litter in Burlington — she had given "Roadside Environment" as a project to one of her students — but this street made Burlington look like a Swiss mountain village. The Store 24 was much as it had been forty years back, when she went there for Twizzlers and Mars bars. Her father had told her never to buy anything there; it would cost twice as much. But what's a Mars bar worth, when you need it now? This morning, she bought cups of ramen in various flavors, cans of soup, a gallon of milk, and a box of granola bars. She didn't check the prices.

Back in the yellow kitchen, she ate a bowl of cereal with a cup of instant coffee, and then she set to work. She started in the basement, packing boxes with stuff that seemed worth keeping—for whose use, she didn't know—and filling black garbage bags with the things that would just have to go. She found grocery bags full of old correspondence—and didn't read it. If she was going to get anything done in five days, she had to be disciplined. This stuff would go straight to the recycling skip at the dump. All the random paraphernalia—old appliances, summer tires, abandoned exercise equipment—would go to a recycling shop. She knew she wasn't supposed to clean, but how could she just leave the wheels of dust behind crates and in corners? She swept. On a shelf by the washer and dryer, she found a paper surgical mask that must have belonged to her father the neurologist. She put it on. Then she apologized to the spiders, and took the broom to the webs that spanned the beams above her. She ran scalding water in the big metal slop sink, rinsed out the unidentifiable gunk, then scrubbed the murky hoppers and the linty shelves.

At noon, she ate a cup of ramen and a chewy granola bar. She had to climb to the second floor for the toilet, because she still hadn't managed to open the powder room door. By evening, the basement was fairly neat, boxes stacked in the middle of the floor. Upstairs, she took a shower behind the water nymph and dried off with one of her mother's fluffy monogrammed towels. In the full-length mirror, she studied her weary body—heavy belly, narrow shoulders, pink mastectomy scar. Then she put on a nightgown she had found in a chest of drawers and fed herself into the sleeping bag on the closet floor. Using a flashlight from a kitchen drawer, she read a little *Alice.* She smiled at the drawing of the little girl grown too big for the rabbit's house, head cramped against the ceiling. Then she slept a dreamless sleep.

Tuesday was warmer, so she decided to work on the garage. God, the garage. A man from a charitable organization came to pick up her mother's SUV, which would be given to a needy family. All the tools and gardening gear—much of it abandoned by her father when he decamped for the city, and never touched again by her mother—she threw in the back of her own car and drove to the recycling shop. The cabinet full of old paint cans and engine oil and windshield wiper fluid required a drive to the hazardous waste depot. Back in the garage, she put on the surgical mask again, and swept up the leafmeal that had accumulated on the floor. In one of her mother's old Smith sweatshirts and a pair of red ski-pants, she must have looked like a lunatic. She was a lunatic. But she was getting things done.

She kept meaning to go buy a new charger—but the time kept evaporating. There was so much to do. And it was all so tiring. After eating some soup and crackers, it was all she could do that evening to sit and gaze around the kitchen, holding the empty soup bowl in both hands.

That night in the closet, she read some more *Alice.* The little girl told the caterpillar that she wasn't sure who she was. The caterpillar didn't seem to care.

On Wednesday she tackled the kitchen. She turned on the radio over the sink, and left it tuned to the dumb pop station. She was tired of hearing about the bloody border wall, anyway. The contact paper on the cupboard shelves was sticky with the residue of decades. Under the refrigerator, the linoleum was as black and gummy as the La Brea tar pits. When she opened the broiler, the door fell off its hinges with a clang, and she spent most of an hour lying on her side, yanking and shoving it, trying to get it back in place. Straining to exert the right leverage, she banged her leg against the floor and was reminded, with a spike of pain, about the scraped spot on her knee. She imagined her mother in just this posture, too stubborn to call a repairman, finally jamming the door shut, broken but out of the way. That's what she did, too.

She ate some soup. She wrapped glasses in old newspaper. She polished the monogrammed silver goblets with the polish she found on the same shelf—and then she worked on the pots and pans, too. It was so satisfying to see the dark metal grow light again. Under the sink, she found a host of solvents and cleaners that required another trip to the hazardous waste depot. She ate some ramen. A granola bar. She took a long soak in the bath. She almost wanted a cigarette. Alice squabbled with the Hatter at the mad tea party.

The days blurred. Ruth put things in boxes. She put things in boxes. She put more things in boxes. She went to get more boxes. How could one person accumulate so much stuff? And why? Ever since her diagnosis, Ruth herself had been de-accessioning, as the museums say.

She wanted to make things easier for whoever would come after.

It must have been Thursday when she got to the living room, the den, the bedrooms. She rolled up carpets and found lagoons of dust beneath. She ran the old vacuum cleaner until its bag was bursting, emptied it, ran it again. She wore the mask, but still found herself coughing for the rest of the day. Alice grew large again at the big trial scene, spilling her fellow jurors out of the jury box, and declared it was all stuff and nonsense.

By Friday morning, Ruth had written nothing. The memorial service would be Saturday at two, so there was still time. She still had work to do in the house. She bundled her mother's wardrobe, sweaters and blouses and underwear, all of it, all of it, off to Goodwill. She marveled at a whole closet full of shoes. Ruth's feet were a size too small. She never found the chinchilla stole.

Oh, the back hall closet. Oh, the chest of drawers in the breezeway, full of miscellaneous stuff. Packets of batteries in various sizes. Shoehorns and birthday candles, faded receipts and business cards, instruction manuals for appliances Ruth had never seen. A whole collection of mysterious keys, none of which worked on the powder room door. Ruth talked to herself as she went. "What is *this* thing for?" "Oh, I remember this!" "Who has *these* anymore?" She almost forgot to eat lunch.

Then, in the drawer of her mother's desk, she found an old address book, and when she leafed through it, a name leaped to her eyes: Essie Hamilton.

Essie was one of the maids who had worked for them back when Ruth was young. Some of those women had come and gone so quickly that Ruth could not now recover their names, but Essie had stayed with the job for years. She didn't have a car, so every morning Ruth's mother drove down to Jeffersonville to pick her up. In summer, when Ruth was out of school, she went along. She remembered the drive into that worn-out neighborhood, under the abandoned train trestle, into a different world, where dark people stood on street corners talking and smoking. When Don and Twyla went out of town for an occasional weekend, Essie spent the night with Ruth, and slept in the master bedroom. With Essie, Ruth got to watch TV at dinner. They ate her spicy shepherd's pie and watched "The Dukes of Hazzard."

This phone number would have been a landline; it had probably been out of use for years. Still, she tried it. It rang several times, and just as she was about to give up, there was the voice she knew, the sharp-edged hello of Essie. Of course she remembered Ruthie. Might she have any time for a little visit this afternoon? She laughed. "My social calendar still has an open spot or two. I'll fit you in before the Queen." She gave Ruth the address.

After hanging up, Ruth realized that she couldn't just show up empty-handed. During her errands this week, she had seen a big new supermarket that was on the way. She drove there.

As a devoted member of her Burlington co-op, Ruth had forgotten what these places were like. It was immense—acres of merchandise under white lights, aisle upon aisle upon aisle. Bright-colored boxes stretched to the vanishing point at the end of each row. She wandered through a section for pets, a drug store, a bakery bigger than any shop in Burlington. It was either wonderful or grotesque. Maybe both.

She drifted to the florist's counter. Most people liked fresh flowers. But Ruth herself hated them. All those green stems, life cut short and then wrapped up with baby's breath in fancy paper with a ribbon, destined to wither in days and be tossed in the trash—it just made her sad. She wandered on.

Somehow she emerged in the dental aisle, surrounded on all sides by stacks of little boxes. Toothpaste for the removal of tartar. Toothpaste for sensitive gums. With baking soda. With mouthwash. Whitening. Extra whitening. Star Wars Bubble-Gum Burst. Tom's of Freaking Maine. All of these products came encased in tubes that would be squeezed and rolled and thrown away, unrecyclable, bound for a landfill, where they would linger forever, mountains of crusty metal to be scaled by future hikers, who would exchange high-fives at the top and smile their impeccable smiles.

Ruth felt dizzy. Her knee throbbed, her head pounded. She made it to the end of the aisle and sat on a pile of plastic sacks filled with peat moss. Why was the Garden Center next to Dental Care? Why did people buy plastic sacks of peat? Plastic sacks of anything? She was short of breath. She was playing croquet with a flamingo. Maybe she had inhaled too much dust this week. She closed her eyes.

And then she started sobbing. Not just crying quietly, but bleating in hiccupping gulps. She tried to stop, and that made her sob harder. Her shoulders shook, her rib-cage seized, the snot streamed down her chin. There was not enough air in this whole huge space. The tears ran and ran. And ran.

The bedroom furniture must have been shoved aside by EMTs. Why did no one set the stool back on its stumpy legs?

When the tears subsided and she could see again, there was a middle-aged man in a red vest standing in front of her. A greeter? A gardener? The store's on-duty therapist? His name tag said "Phil." He didn't say anything. But he also didn't leave. Sobbing on the peat moss was probably against store policy. Ruth shrugged at him, then got up and wandered off.

She found herself in kitchenware, and a memory returned. Once, when she was about ten, she had decided to get Essie a Christmas present. The thing she chose, the thing she could afford, was a single drinking glass made of green plastic. It never struck her that this was odd; it just seemed like the right thing. Essie welcomed the unexpected gift with a delighted smile. Now, Ruth found a whole section devoted to cups and glasses, most of them in plastic-wrapped bundles of a dozen or fifty. Those would never do. But here was a single plastic cup, apparently a display model. She picked it up and hurried to the express check-out. The cashier looked perplexed, but there was a bar code, so all was well. Ruth said she didn't need a bag—and the cashier stuffed the cup into a bag anyway. Ruth pulled it out and handed the bag back to the poor woman. No lecture was needed. Ruth's eyes were red, her cheeks tear-stained and puffy. Life was hard enough already. Bearing her chalice into the vast parking lot, she lit out for Essie's.

She could have made that drive blindfolded. Down the hill, through a shabby little business district, under the train trestle, decorated now with more vivid tags than in her memory. Did that say "I Am The Flim-Flam Man"? She turned into a web of streets lined by two- and three-story wood-frame homes without any yards to speak of. Tottering front porches hung just above the sidewalks. Three or four mailboxes were nailed by each front door. This was the same neighborhood where Essie had lived years ago. At least there was a little late-afternoon light to brighten it today.

After a long wait, the doorbell was answered by a dark-skinned black man who looked to be in his late forties. She thought she must have made a mistake—but he said, "Are you Ruthie?"

"Ruth," she said. "And you?"

"John," he said, and ushered her in. Ruth remembered, as she followed him up the narrow stair to the second-floor apartment, that Essie had a son. Ruth had never met him, but once in a while Essie mentioned her boy. When she spent the night with Ruth, she left him with his grandmother. This boy, now a man about Ruth's age, led her into a dim kitchen where a laptop sat open on the table. Ruth was tempted to ask if she could check her e-mail. Instead, she handed him the cup.

He looked down at it and asked if she would like something to drink.

"Oh, no, thanks, I'm good."

"All right, then," he said, and led her down a dark hallway. Over his shoulder he said, "Mom doesn't see much now, but she hears every damn thing."

"I heard that," said a voice from the room they were entering, on the back of the building. Two windows looked out on the buildings behind. She was seated in a wheelchair in the middle of the largely empty room. There was no carpet, just a green sofa against one wall and a large flat-screen TV against the other. The woman in the wheel chair was tiny. Ruth remembered that Essie had cut a trim figure in her white maid's dress, but the person before her was a wisp that almost disappeared into the chair. Her close-cropped hair was iron-gray, under a little red cloche that must have been pinned on. Her skin was coffee and cream.

John excused himself; he had work to do. His mother said, "If I need to go out, he carries me. First the chair, then me. But I don't go out much. I've got everything I need in this house." In the bare room, her voice rang like a wind chime.

"It's so good of you to visit," she said. "I heard about your mother. I'm sorry. She was a nice lady."

Ruth thanked her, and asked about her health.

"Oh, I'm all right," she said. "I'd like to see better. I'd like to walk. But I'd like to fly, too, and that's not happening. Now, if they were to take away my mouth, *that* would be a problem." She laughed. "But how are *you*?"

"Well, I'm trying to clean up the house, you know?"

"Oh, honey, you and Hercules."

Ruth laughed. "So I'm pretty tired. I've discovered some muscles I didn't know I had. But it's all right. I even sort of like it."

Essie hummed in sympathy, and Ruth went on.

"The other day," she said, "I met some of my mother's friends. From her church."

"Her *church*? You mean the synagogue?"

"No, her church. United Methodist."

"United Methodist. OK. It takes all kinds."

"And they said something about her painting."

"You mean like *picture* painting?"

"Watercolors. Landscapes. Did you ever see her painting?"

"Only when she painted the kitchen that god-awful yellow. Your father like to have a fit."

They laughed again, and Ruth said, "It's good to talk. You know?"

Essie nodded.

"Why couldn't I talk like this with my mother?"

Essie paused, then said, "Your mother was terrified of you."

"What?"

"You were so smart, so—verbal. Even at five years

old, you were talking up a storm. You told us about your friends at school, and their pets, and the stories the teacher read to you, and the lessons you were learning. I remember a whole project you did about the creatures of the sea, because you told us all about it."

"I did?"

"The midnight zone. The hatchet-head shark. You showed us pictures. That was one ugly fish. You told us your dreams, in all their weird details. Sometimes it was too much information, I swear." She laughed. "And your mother, she wasn't like that. You know? I think she thought a lady keeps certain things to herself. She didn't know what to do with you."

They both fell silent. The room was getting darker. After a minute, Ruth said, "Oh, about the house."

"Yes?"

"I haven't been able to get into the powder room. You know, the downstairs bathroom?"

"Oh, I know. Your mother always called it the powder room. Did you look over the door?"

"Over the door?"

"Just run your hand along that lintel. Certain people were sometimes known to lock themselves into that powder room, so she kept a key up there."

John reappeared at the door, and flipped on the wall switch, which lit a single lamp. He said, "Don't keep your guest sitting in the dark, Mom."

"I didn't hear anyone complaining."

He said, "Ruth, I'm fixing supper. Can you stay?"

She said no, she couldn't. Essie didn't want to take no for an answer, but Ruth said she had work to do. She kissed Essie on the cheek, and John led her back down the hall.

Pulling on her coat in the kitchen, she thanked him. He nodded, and she said, "It's wonderful how you look after your mother."

"She changed my diapers," he said.

She said she would show herself out, and he let her.

She had to put a box under the powder room door in order to reach. When she ran her hand up there, it brought down a curl of dust. And a little wire key.

The old wall switch made a clunking sound, and the overhead light blinked on. It was the bathroom she remembered — black-and-white-tiled floor, shiny white tiled walls with the black diamond motif, a sturdy old sink that stood on its own porcelain pedestal. There was room for a soft settee under the wavy-glass window, and now, in the early evening, darkness beyond. Along the windowless wall facing the sink, stacked against the towel rods, there was a collection of paintings. Six of them, all on canvas stretched over wooden frames, all in different sizes. An easel stood in front of the settee, holding another canvas. On the closed toilet lay a palette and several brushes; on a board laid across the sink was a selection of paints in metal tubes. The mirror on the medicine cabinet bore a curly mustache in black paint, just at the right height for Ruth. It suited her astonished face.

With her own shadow in the way of the stark overhead light, she couldn't see the paintings as well as she'd like — but she could see that they were all variations on a theme. Pale backgrounds in a thick impasto of cream or lavender, with a horizon line across the middle, where the color shifted slightly, growing lighter toward the top. Were they beach scenes? This house was only ten miles from the shore — but they had hardly ever gone there when Ruth was growing up. Too much traffic, too much trouble, too much sand and sunburn. In some of the pictures, there were suggestions of dunes or sea grasses, gestured at so faintly that you couldn't be sure. The canvas on the easel showed a dim gray V in the sky — if that *was* the sky — which might be a seabird on the wing. But it seemed to have been painted over; it was barely visible. Maybe that picture was still unfinished.

Maybe they all were. Maybe that was why they were all here, locked into this makeshift studio, unready to meet the world. In a gallery, Ruth would have passed them without lingering. They might have been good for the halls of some mid-level seaside hotel. Or a living room like Taffy's.

But still. They were her mother's. Ruth sat on the settee for a long time, and stared.

Then she fixed a cup of ramen, and stood at the kitchen window, looking at the lights of the neighbors behind. She still hadn't written a word. And she didn't feel up to it now. She just wanted to crawl into her sleeping bag. In the morning, she would go to Best Buy, get a charger, and bang out what she had to say in a coffee shop.

But when morning came, she didn't want to leave the house. It was more or less in order — carpets rolled up and leaning against bare walls, boxes stacked in the middle of floors. She could finish the work tomorrow, before picking up Harper in the city and driving back to Vermont. But she kept finding more things to do. In the brightness of the first sunny day all week, she saw spots that needed spackle, windowsills too dusty to leave unscrubbed. The powder room needed attention, of course — the medicine cabinet, the linen closet, the paint-spotted floor. She stacked the paintings on the front porch. Maybe the Auxes would be interested. Then she went back inside, where she shussed around the echoing rooms, always finding more to do.

Speaking impromptu had never been her style. For classes, she always had a thorough lesson plan, with all the statistics and the lines she wanted to quote. She stood in awe of colleagues who spoke well extempore — but also in exasperation at those who bumbled on as if no one's time was precious. Even for meetings and rallies, she had to have notes at hand; without them, she feared that she would freeze while everyone was watching. And yet, for her mother's funeral, apparently, she was going to wing it.

She didn't get to the church early, as she had planned. She barely had time to change into a dark pant suit and rush to the car, where she counted on GPS to get her there. In the pale blue of a clear sky, she saw the setting moon, faint as a vaccination mark.

It being Saturday, the parking lot was largely empty. Ruth hurried to the main door of the big red brick church with its white steeple shining in the sun. There was no one in the narthex; everyone must already be seated. Striding across the carpeted floor, she had misgivings about the pant suit—but it was too late now. Then a door opened in front of her, and she heard a familiar voice: "Ruthie! Thank goodness you're here!"

Taffy was resplendent in a black satin dress. "We saved a seat for you up front."

Not that seats needed to be saved: the great barn of a building was empty, except for three pews near the front. The sun streamed in through the high, clear windows, bathing the space in light. At the foot of the steps to the sanctuary, a dark casket gleamed. Who would the pallbearers be?

Taffy led her to a seat in the first pew, and within seconds the minister rose to her lectern. Had they been waiting for Ruth? The next person over, another seventyish woman in black, handed her a program with a solemn smile. There was her mother, in a recent head shot, eyes focused earnestly somewhere beyond the camera. Beneath it, centered in white space, was Frost's "The Road Less Traveled." Could that have been her mother's choice? Or did they just put it on every memorial program?

The pipe organ boomed. The minister raised her arms like gleaming white wings, and everybody stood. They sang "Amazing Grace." The woman next to Ruth was especially full-throated, a husky contralto. It was awful. At that very moment, in memorial services all over America, people were singing that dreadful song. Her mother was not a wretch. Where were the Captain and Tennille when you needed them?

The minister quoted some scripture. It was printed on the back of the program, but Ruth couldn't make her eyes work. Then she heard her own name, and looked up. The minister gestured to her with an open palm, then sat behind a little wooden wall. Ruth made her way to the lectern.

Up here, the room looked even brighter. The winter sun stared through the western windows, lighting up every face. There was Taffy and a whole pew full of Auxes; those new faces must be Frieda and Sukie. There was her father, his head tilted like a tacking sloop, his frizzy curls grayer and thinner than when she had seen him last. Beside him sat Harper, long yellow locks glowing against a dark dress. In the aisle, sitting in her own chair and wearing a black beret, there was Essie, a small dark flame. In the pew beside her, wearing a dark suit and a gleaming white shirt, there was John, gazing, like everyone else, at Ruth.

She looked for a moment out the tall windows. A shoal of birds rose and whirled, calling to each other. Something calmed her. She gripped the lectern with both hands. And then she spoke.

Things We Said Today

He didn't mean to get into a relationship. That was the whole point about leaving his marriage—being unfettered, keeping his options open. He had left behind a welt that he tried not to think about—a husbandless wife, a fatherless daughter. Getting into a new relationship would make a mockery of it all. And yet here he was, walking out of Clea's bedroom into her living room, where her fifteen-year-old son sat on the sofa, absorbed in his laptop. Clea herself stood at the stove in the open-plan kitchen, frying bacon. It smelled like home. Not his home, but somebody's. He wondered if she was still pissed off.

It was New Year's Day, 2017. The night before, they had gone dancing. This wasn't Mac's idea; he danced like Joe Cocker, and preferred not to impose that on the world. But what were they going to do in Saint Johnsbury on New Year's Eve? He didn't know anyone there, and he wasn't eager to be stuck at some party with her friends. So when she suggested dancing at the VFW Hall, he thought why not. It would probably be similar to some scenes he had witnessed growing up outside of Bristol.

It was better. There was a live band, and it wasn't playing covers of Journey. It was a spunky acoustic trio doing old-timey bluegrass—the Stanley Brothers, Bill Monroe. On the upright bass was a tall bald dude who looked like he read P. G. Wodehouse aloud to his insomniac wife. They lolloped through a loose-limbed waltz, and Clea dragged Mac around the sparsely populated linoleum floor. Strings of left-over Christmas lights blinked red and green on the walls.

Clea was pretty, in an old-fashioned way. Her pale red hair fell in two sheets from a central part to her shoulders, where it curled in a brief gesture at stylishness. She wore a forest-green crew-neck sweater, a grey flannel skirt, and knee socks. She swore that her knees never got cold. At six foot three, Mac loomed over her, hawklike and ruddy. His sandy hair, thinning on top, could use a trim in back. He wore his cleanest cargo pants and a mushroom-colored sweater that had lost its shape long ago. He did the hokey-pokey and he shook it all about.

At 9:30 they clicked plastic cups of seltzer and made believe it was midnight. They had to pick up her son before the bowling alley closed.

"I never liked champagne anyway," she said. "And A.A. definitely doesn't like it." She chugged her seltzer and emitted a satisfied sigh. "Sorry this isn't more glamorous. But this is what you get when your date is a 43-year-old recovering divorcee."

"What are you recovering from?" he asked.

"What do you got?"

Mac laughed. He was somewhere close to happy.

The bowling alley smelled of popcorn with a hint of lager. Its carpeted central area, with the bar and the counter for multicolored shoes, was dimly lit, but the bright lanes glowed in the distance. Thunder rolled, and small detonations clattered up and down the line. They found Philippe as he was wrapping up his last game. On his final ball, he bowled a strike from the Brooklyn side. That wasn't supposed to happen, but when you hurled the ball as hard as Philippe did, all bets were off.

Philippe was a big dude. Not fat, exactly, just large all over, from his big head of dark curls to his size fourteens. You could set a brimming cup and saucer safely on the plane of his shoulder. He clapped a high five with a teammate, then joined his mother and Mac at the bar. Mac offered to buy him a cookie from a big glass container.

"No thanks, Mr. McKenzie. Those things are lethal."

"Call me Mac. They don't look so bad."

The boy pointed to a hand-lettered notice taped to the side of the jar. "MAY CONTAIN NUTS!"

"Oh, jeez, sorry."

"That's OK, you couldn't know."

Clea said, "He's very good at watching out for himself."

Philippe said, "Well, I don't want my head to swell to twice its normal size. It's big enough already."

Mac didn't know if he should laugh. Clea asked him, "Are you allergic to anything?"

"Shellfish and Republicans."

Philippe snorted. Clea didn't say anything. That line always got a laugh in Burlington. When the silence continued, he said, "But seriously, some of my best friends are Republicans." He didn't know any Republicans. Philippe shot him a look. Mac said, "That was a heck of a final ball you bowled."

Philippe turned to his mother, who was fussing with the frayed sleeve of his enormous red-and-white letter jacket. "We gotta go, Mom. They're closing."

The ride home was quiet, and so was the bedroom. OK, it was a dumb joke. But jeez.

When Mac emerged from the bedroom on New Year's Day, Philippe looked up and nodded, then turned back to his laptop. Across the room, Clea focused on the bacon, with ABBA on the iPod. Mac lingered in between them, at the window in the yellow dining nook, which looked out on a frozen little yard. She set a mug for him on the breakfast bar, then returned to the stovetop. The coffee was delicious; she had steamed the milk.

She shouldn't let her son spend so much time online. It would stunt his communication skills. Probably already had. Mac and Ruth had always limited Harper's screen time; that was one thing they did right.

Back in Burlington this morning, there would be no bacon frying. Ruth did not believe in bacon. The fat. The nitrates. The poor pigs. She would already be at work on her laptop, whacking out e-mails, posting communiqués, probably organizing a Women's March for Burlington on Inauguration Day. Ruth thought globally and acted locally. Clea fried bacon and sang along to "Waterloo."

She scrambled eggs and served them with toast and hot sauce. Philippe hoovered his food and went back to his laptop. His mother suggested they go for a drive. Maybe last night's little storm had passed.

Clea Lagarde owned the only stationery shop in Saint Johnsbury. It was a little too frou-frou for her taste—too much pastel, too many cards that said "I Love You Forever"—but that was what people expected from a historic red-brick building on Park Street. There was no way she could compete with the online guys on office supplies. And she was going to compete, by God.

Her ex-husband was long gone—back to his people in Quebec. He probably never should have tried settling with the Yankee girl he met in college. But sometimes you don't know until you try. He sent occasional e-mails, and skyped with Philippe once a week. He wasn't a bad man, just a distant one.

Philippe was her gem, her rock, her worry. Like his father, he had always been big. One day in grade school, he had come home to report that the other kids were calling him The Bus. She started to call his teacher, to express her outrage—but he said, "No! I *am* The Bus!" Just last week, when she had called him from his bedroom, shouting, "Bus, dinner's ready!" Mac had said, "Isn't that kind of a rough nickname?" She said, "You think he doesn't know he's big?"

Mac could be sensitive like that. Which was good, she guessed. On OKCupid, he had said he was "in his very late youth." He also said he had never been married, and that seemed good, too—no ex, no alimony, no kids clamoring for attention, or rejecting it. But she remembered her mother saying once, back in days of yore, that if a man hasn't been married by thirty, there has to be a reason.

He said he was in transition, having arrived in the area just a few weeks before. He was living out of his truck—just for a while—but he was clean and polite and well-spoken. He liked playing cribbage. He seemed to want what she wanted—companionship, sex, someone to talk to. His interest in sports perplexed her, as always—why do grown men care about squads of men who happen to wear the name of certain cities or colleges on their chests? But that might be a price she could pay. He was fine with Philippe—not trying too hard, not a back-slapping dad wannabe. A little tentative, maybe. She took that as a sign of respect, the way you behave with someone you don't know yet.

She liked taking drives in her old powder-blue Camry. There were some rattles under the hood, and the upholstery smelled like tuna casserole, but the heater worked, and the radio. How much does a person need?

Every New Year's Day, a local station played nothing

but the Beatles. Just now, John was intoning "Norwegian Wood." Philippe was wedged into the back seat, focused on his phone. The highway was windswept and bare. You could ride it from here to Gloccamorra. Mac was quiet. She decided to go for it.

"Why did you leave — whatever you left?"

He shifted his weight in the seat. "It was just time to move on." Then he was quiet again.

Some gray and white fields scrolled by. She hated the word "just." People used it all the time — to minimize, to elide, to delete. I was just wondering. I just have to get back to my people. It's just the way things are.

When Ringo launched into "Octopus's Garden," she remembered that the Beatles thing was alphabetical. What song came next? You could play this game all day. She put her money on "Oh! Darling."

Should she let him get away with this? How much did she want his company?

The sun was a pale smudge on a mottled sky. "Oh! Darling" it was.

Mac knew he should have said more. But with Philippe in the back seat? With a whole new year beginning? Gray and white fields scrolled by. Paul reminisced about Penny Lane. Very strange. Eventually, he spoke.

"Back when I was in high school, my parents took me and my brother on a vacation to Italy. It was the only time they ever left the country. They ran a farm; they didn't have time to gallivant. But it was winter, and they got someone to feed the animals. They had to do this now, before it would be too late. My mother wanted to see the Mediterranean. It was as if they knew—although they didn't know yet—that in five years she would be dead from a sudden tumor. I didn't want to go, but I didn't have any choice.

"Most of the trip was a blur, train stations and loud restaurants. People speaking English because they wanted your money. My father's forced cheerfulness, my brother being a know-it-all. Who cared why the tower was leaning? We took my mother to the beach at Viareggio on a gray day in December, when there was no one around. She dipped a foot in the sea. I've forgotten just about all the rest of it.

"Except for one thing. A church in Venice. It wasn't one of the famous ones. I remember it was off the tourist track, out on one edge of the city. You could smell the salty sewage smell of the lagoon, and there were seagulls hovering around. It had an impressive white stone façade, but so many buildings had grown up around it that you didn't realize at first how big it was. You stepped inside, and suddenly you were in this cavernous space with a high vaulted ceiling and a long central aisle receding into shadows. Not far from the entrance, some candles were burning, and an old woman in black knelt in front of them.

"Somehow, I got detached from my family and wandered alone to the front of the sanctuary. There was no one around. On the left, there was an unmarked door. I stepped through it, and found myself in this little separate chapel, just big enough for about ten people to stand on the stone floor. But it was empty when I walked in. It was cold in there, and dark; there was just one stained-glass window. But I could see a marble altar on the wall, and above the altar a painting. In front of it, there was a rail that supported a metal box, and a plaque with instructions in several languages. The box had a slot for coins. I put one in, and a shutter went thwack, and a bright light shone on the painting. In the box, a motor whirred—a timer on the light."

He let some fields go by. She didn't say anything. Philippe must still be focused on his phone. The Beatles cried Please Mister Postman. Mac went on.

"The painting was a Madonna and child, with four men standing around them. The plaque said they were saints. I didn't know at the time, but later I learned that one of them was Saint Sebastian, because he had several arrows through his torso. You know, that's how they always show Sebastian."

She nodded, eyes on the road.

"Sebastian was looking right at me, and he seemed completely—unperturbed. Like this was something that happened every day. Like, what arrows? I don't remember who the other saints were. Behind this little group, there was a hazy green landscape—rolling hills, deer grazing, a castle in the distance. It was like a fairy world, a place that the people in the picture would never know.

"Of course, the center of the painting was supposed to be the baby Jesus, standing there in all his naked glory on his mother's knee. But I thought the real center was Mary. She was wearing a dark blue dress. And she looked — satisfied. It was like she was saying, I did this.

"Suddenly, the light clicked off, and the little room went dark again. I wanted more than anything to look at that picture some more. But I didn't have any more coins, and I wasn't going to ask for any. I said to myself, That's all you get, so deal with it. I left that room, and rejoined my family, and probably got a lecture about going off on my own. I don't remember.

"Later, I looked the picture up, and read about the painter. Giovanni Bellini. He spent his whole life in Venice. The scholars said he had a reputation for kindness. His best-known paintings, which hung in the Doge's Palace, were destroyed in a fire. This particular painting wasn't famous. It came from 1507, when he was seventy-seven years old. He died eight years later.

"I found reproductions of the painting in art books, and, later, on the Internet — but they never looked much like the picture I had seen. The saint with the arrows going through him, gazing right at you. The deer walking in the hills. That proud young woman with the baby on her knees."

He stopped talking. The Beatles were up to Rocky Raccoon.

He didn't say, That's why I left my home. Because who would understand that?

Somewhere between Stowe and Saint J, he looked over and saw that Clea was silently crying. He couldn't stand it.

"I'm sorry," he said. "That thing I said last night was just a dumb joke. I didn't mean to upset you."

She shook her head, keeping her eyes on the road. A tear slid down her cheek.

"Clea, I'm sorry. I was just—"

From the back seat came the voice of The Bus. "Mr. McKenzie? My mother needs her space right now."

She Said She Said. Strawberry Fields. Things We Said Today.

Nocturne

Naturally, it is night. At the kitchen table on Louise Street, all three of them are sitting in the yellow glow of the hanging lamp. Mother, father, full-grown daughter. Outside, in the little back yard, the roaring dark.

So much, in their lives, had taken place at night. It was night when Harper was born, as Mac and the midwife looked on, unable to ease Ruth's pain. In the years that followed, Ruth got most of her work done at night, in her study after dinner, preparing the next day's classes, catching up on e-mail. It was always night when Harper refused to sleep, when she wandered the house and hectored her parents until one of them, usually Mac, paid her some attention. Night was the hardest time during the treatment of Ruth's cancer, when she stood at the sink with a cup of hot milk that she couldn't swallow and wondered about the world. After her first recovery, night was the time of Mac's untakebackable moment, when he set his housekeys on the kitchen counter along with a note saying that his departure would be best for all of them, and then rolled out the driveway in his truck, taking their old dog with him. Night, of course, was when Harper slipped out to see Josh, the older boy who made her feel alive. And it was on an ordinary night, two months ago, that Ruth got the call from her father: her mother had died. It is impossible that any of these things could have happened in the light of day.

It will be night when Ruth dies. At least, that's how she imagines it. Who dies at three in the afternoon?

It is late April, Holy Week and Passover. The stores are full of chocolate bunnies. The homeless guys are back full-time in City Hall Park, sitting on the bench by the fountain, laughing their ratchety laughs. The season holds its breath.

Mother, father, and daughter sit at the kitchen table, in the yellow glow. They have not been together since he left. Ruth is imposing conditions.

"You have to get rid of that truck."

"What?" This isn't where he thought it would start.

"It's an eyesore. It's too loud. It's a gas hog."

"But—"

"What kind of mileage does it get?"

"Well—"

"That's what I thought. It was already a pollution bomb six years ago."

Any reference to six years ago shuts him up quickly. She goes on.

"You don't think we're going to sleep together, do you?"

He looks at Harper. This tall young woman, this shape-shifter, who used to be The Bean. Are they really going to discuss this in front of their daughter? She may be nineteen, but still. Harper arcs her eyebrows at him. Apparently, they are.

"Um, no."

"Good. You can use the study."

She must see the surprise on his ruddy face. She says, "I just buried my mother. I'm not in the business of turning people away."

She puts a hand on his forearm—the first time she has touched him since his return. Her dark eyes flare up behind her black-framed glasses.

"You know I'm dying, right?"

"Mom—"

"Harper doesn't like it when I talk this way. But we need to speak truth now. You know about my health?"

"I know you're back in treatment." He learned this back in February, when he sat with Harper in a café near the restaurant where she works, and she told him he had to leave. He didn't blame her. He had no right to return. He did leave, for a while: he drove down to Addison County to visit his brother, thinking he might stay there. But that was another misfire. He had to come back here.

Ruth nods. "And you know I don't want pity."

"Oh, yeah," he says. "Heaven help the fool who tries to pity you."

A little smile lights her pale round face. "All right, then," she says.

Nobody asks why he left, where he's been, why he's back. He has been rehearsing his explanations for months, walking the streets of the Old North End, picking up litter as he went. Nobody asks about Sloppy Joe. Just as well.

He doesn't know what he'll do. He can't resume his old job at the university library. There are only so many burned bridges you can cross again. One thing at a time.

Ruth gets up. She looks tired. "I have a crazy amount of work to do," she says. But she doesn't seem as worried about it as the old Ruth would have been. She heads upstairs.

Mac and Harper remain at the table. He gazes off into the dark. He can feel her looking at the side of his face. What does she see? After a minute, she gets up, too, but stops before leaving the room.

"No Cheez-Doodles in the study," she says, and leaves him at the table.

The next day, he takes the truck to the Subaru dealer and sells it, just like that. He'd get a better deal if he posted it online and fielded offers, but a better deal is not in the cards right now. It's like pulling off a Band-Aid. It's like the death of Sloppy Joe. It's like being forty-eight in a world designed for youth.

He walks home, on a cold morning and finds Ruth still in her study, preparing for her afternoon class. Last night's fatigue has given way to a flush of fresh activity. She is typing madly at her laptop, cell phone wedged against one ear. "See you tonight!" she says into it, then sets it down.

"What's up?" Mac asks.

She gives him her hurried-but-happy look. "You know the plan for City Hall Park?"

He nods. Even before he left, there were complaints about vagrants and drugs.

"They're starting the renovation," she says. "They ignored our protests about cutting down trees. They rejected the thousands of signatures we gathered to put it on the ballot. Now they're about to ruin our only downtown green space, closing it for at least a year, cutting down trees, pouring more cement, putting in a profit-making kiosk, and displacing the Farmer's Market, not to mention the people who use that space daily for recreation."

"You mean the homeless guys."

"They have a right to public space, too. You know who owns the park?"

"Um, the city?"

"No. The people."

"OK."

"In the proposal for the renovation, you know who they say they're serving?"

"Let me guess. Not the people."

She puts a finger to the tip of her nose. Then she raises both hands for air quotes. "'The stakeholders,'" she says. "By which they mean the suburbanites and tourists who'll come and buy their seven-dollar cappuccinos."

"So? What are you going to do?"

"You'll see," she says.

She glances at the clock on her laptop and says, "Shit."

She starts collecting her papers, stuffing them into a worn canvas bag. "I've got a bus to catch."

"I'll drive you," he says. "In your car. If that's OK."

She used to drive herself, but she has been trying to use the car less. She starts to say no, but they both know that the bus trip requires a transfer downtown, and a ride will save her thirty precious minutes of prep time. His life as a chauffeur begins.

In the car, she asks, "What are you doing for money?"

"I just sold the truck."

"Well, that should cover about two weeks of beer."

He winces, but doesn't speak. On the radio, there's something about the Mueller Report. In ten years, no one will know what the Mueller Report was. When he pulls up to the curb in front of her building, she lingers before getting out.

"I'll find my own way home."

"I could pick you up," he says.

"I don't know when it will be. I've got some work to do downtown. I'll take the shuttle. I bet someone will drive me home after that."

"OK," he says.

"Spend some time with Harper," she says. "If she'll let you."

When he gets back to the house, he finds Harper in the kitchen, grabbing a snack before going to hang out with Josh.

Mac says, "The guy from Jackson Terrace?"

"Yeah." She spreads almond butter on a cracker and stuffs the whole thing in her mouth. Jackson Terrace is the apartment complex just down the hill from their neighborhood.

"Is he still a big skateboarder?"

She points to her mouth — too full to speak — but nods.

"Are you two, like, boyfriend and girlfriend?"

She chews for a moment, then says, "We're not into labels."

"I see."

She prepares another cracker and fills her mouth again.

"So," he says, "What's he doing these days?"

Again, she chews, then says, "They're still working with their father. Construction."

Mac cocks his head. "'They'?"

"Josh uses the pronouns 'they' and 'them' now."

"But he's still a guy, right?"

"They don't identify with the gender binary anymore."

"But—"

"Dad, I don't think you're going to get it." She re-seals the box of crackers.

Mac can't help himself. "Does he have a penis or not?"

She screws on the lid of the almond butter. "I gotta go," she says.

"I'll give you a ride."

"No, thanks. The bus is easy." And she's out the door.

That night, Mac is on his own. He sits in the study, in the old reading chair. It used to be *his* study, where he watched ballgames and read books about Antarctic expeditions. In another lifetime. Tonight, he finds a magazine article about recent initiatives to colonize the moon. Just this January, the Chinese landed an unmanned craft—the first time anyone has landed on the far side of the moon, the side we never see. He learns that on that side there is a mountain peak taller than Mount Everest. There's a crater that's more than four miles deep. He loves this stuff. The article says that the moon is drifting away from the Earth at a rate of four centimeters a year. The lunar night lasts for fourteen of our days. Probes have found evidence of H_2O, and already people are planning to market moonwater. Harper used to be interested in the moon. He'll tell her about it tomorrow.

He hears the women of the house come in, hears them go about their business in the kitchen, in the hall. They settle. The house settles. The moon drifts. He goes on reading.

The next morning in the kitchen, he finds a note in Ruth's handwriting: "We're at City Hall Park. Don't worry about us for meals." Her car is in the driveway. They must have taken the bus. He decides to walk the mile into town and see what's up.

When he gets there, the park is in a stand-off. On one side is a crew of four guys in neon-yellow nylon vests, each of them holding a chainsaw. Wearing sonic ear muffs and big plastic goggles, they look like giant space-bugs from a sci-fi movie.

The other side is more diffuse. At every tree throughout the park, there's a person chained to the trunk with a bike-lock cable threaded through belt loops and cinched with a padlock. It looks like every student from Environmental Studies 101 has answered the call. Chained to a maple near Main Street, there's Ruth's old friend Silverman, with whom Mac used to work in the library. And up by the steps to City Hall, Harper and Josh are padlocked to neighboring locusts, sitting cross-legged and chatting. Ruth is circulating with a sack of bagels.

Around the fountain in the center of the park, a crowd has gathered. Someone from *Seven Days* is jotting on a notepad. A camera crew is setting up. At their usual bench, six or seven homeless guys are holding wooden stakes. A couple of them spar with each other, making light-sabre sounds. One tall man in a dark green hoodie starts pounding his stake on the sidewalk and declaiming in a big brassy voice, "Hell no, we won't go!" The rest of the men start pounding and chanting along.

Mac sidles up to Silverman, who greets him as if he had never been away. "McKenzie!" he says, and pats the patchy grass beside him. He's a wiry guy with silver-framed glasses and a graying ponytail. "Have a seat, man. Sorry all the trees are taken. Shit should be going down soon."

Mac sits beside him and says, "What's the plan?"

"Well, either we're going to have the biggest chainsaw massacre in the history of Vermont, or the forces of good will triumph." He looks at his phone. "We've sent a demand to the Mayor, telling him to call off the dogs. Look at those guys." He gazes over at the city workers, who are huddled on the little plaza in back of the old firehouse. "What a bunch of tools."

Mac says, "They're just trying to do a job. I kinda feel bad for them."

"Oh, don't worry about them, man. They're on the clock, whether they do any sawing or not. On the taxpayer's dime, of course." Silverman looks over at City Hall. "Hey, looks like we've got some action. It's Mayor McSmiley Face!"

Down the steps of City Hall comes the handsome young mayor, wearing a dark sportscoat but no tie. From the bottom step he surveys the scene, his gaze lingering on Ruth, who is standing near the fountain. The homeless guys chant louder. The reporter and the camera crew head toward the Mayor, but he seems to want no part of them. He looks at the city workers and makes a sawing motion with one hand across his throat, then turns and goes back up the steps and into City Hall.

"Did you see that?" says Silverman. "Did he just give the order to kill us all?"

Mac laughs. "I think that meant 'cease and desist.'"

"Oh," says Silverman. He sounds disappointed. "Well, I guess that's good."

The city guys gather their equipment and stalk off toward their van, accompanied by a chorus of gleeful profanities from the homeless men. As the van pulls away, a cheer goes up from all around the park.

Turning toward Harper and Josh, Mac sees that they are not sharing in the jubilation. Harper is staring at the central plaza, and the look on her face is stricken. Mac follows her gaze. There by the fountain, Ruth is lying in a heap.

By the time Mac reaches her, three of the homeless guys are gathered over her body, which they have stretched out on the sidewalk. The tall man with the green hoodie has taken it off, rolled it up, and placed it under her head. She is breathing but unconscious. The hoodie man says, "We've got to get her to the ER."

Mac doesn't have a car. Harper, Josh, and Ruth arrived on foot. Silverman came down from campus on the shuttle bus. They start looking for a student with a car.

The hoodie man says, "We'll take the bus." He looks at his watch. "It stops fifty yards from here every fifteen minutes, and runs right to the front door of the hospital. It should pass any minute." He says to one of his companions, "Go make sure it doesn't leave before we get there."

Mac says, "I'm her husband." The hoodie man says, "Take a leg."

Just after three o'clock that afternoon, the doctor comes out to find them in the ER waiting room. Mac, Harper, Josh, and Silverman are all sitting in a row; off to the side are four of the homeless guys. The hoodie man has put his sweatshirt back on. His name, it turns out, is Rowan.

The doctor's lab coat flaps with her gestures as she speaks to this congregation.

"She's resting."

Eight sets of shoulders relax a little. The doctor surveys the whole group, and allows herself a smile. "I feel like I'm teaching a class." Then she goes on. "It's hard to say what the immediate problem is. I mean, we know she's been weakened by chemo and radiation; we know the cancer is advancing. But the scans don't show anything that would knock her out like this. Unless she was overtired, anyway."

Everybody nods.

"We'll keep her overnight. Tomorrow, if everything checks out OK, she should be able to go home. That's usually the best place to recover. Can you keep her from over-exerting herself?"

She addresses this question to Mac. Mac looks at Harper. Harper looks at Silverman. Silverman looks at Josh. Josh shrugs.

Rowan says, "We'll take care of it."

It's not the kind of thing you can take care of. But somebody had to say something.

That night after visiting hours, Mac and Harper and Josh are back in the kitchen on Louise Street. Josh is making a salad. They made a stop at City Market for provisions on their way back into town. Josh is at the sink, washing butter lettuce. Harper is standing at the counter, too, cutting hearts of Romaine on the bias. Her iPod plays some trancey dance music, like bagpipes on uppers. Mac is sitting at the table, and Josh is talking hockey.

"You should've seen it, Mr. McKenzie. The Bs were short-handed, they were killing a penalty, you know, Marchand got caught for one of those dumb high-checking moves, so they should have been sitting back, but Tyler got out in front with the puck, you know, he's a rookie, he doesn't know any better, and the goalie came out of the crease to meet him because it looked like he was going to shoot, but at the last second he flipped the puck off to his left, and suddenly there was Bergeron with an empty net in front of him, and he just popped it in like they were doing a warm-up drill. It was sweet. My old man jumped out of his skin."

Mac says, "Wow." As an old Vermonter, he is supposed to care about hockey. In fact, everything Josh just said might as well have been spoken in Swahili. But "Wow" is enough.

At the cutting board, Harper minces a shallot. "This is the best salad in the world," she says. "Four kinds of greens—butter, Romaine, endive, and watercress—plus shallots, plus thyme."

Josh shakes the shoulder-length dark hair out of their face and puts a load of lettuce in a salad spinner. "You have to wash each of the greens three times," they say. "Once in luke-warm water, once in cool water, and once in cold."

Harper picks up a jar from the counter and shakes it. "And this is the best dressing ever."

Mac says, "What's so great about the dressing?"

"Oh," says Josh, "a special ingredient."

"Yeah?"

Harper says, "A teaspoon of warm water! Can you believe it? People think a vinaigrette is so sacred, like, you'd never want to dilute it—but people are wrong!" She holds up the jar. "This stuff is so good you'll want to drink it neat."

Josh presses the final leafy greens dry with a dish-towel and starts laying them on dinner plates. "You've got to drizzle the dressing on one layer at a time." Harper, poised with the jar, obliges. "That coats the leaves enough but not too much."

They pile the lettuces high on all three plates and bring them to the table. The hopped-up pipes play on. Outside, the lunar dark. Each time a person moves, the windows reflect new lights.

Up on the hill, Ruth is resting quietly. Tomorrow, with no one to lead the wood fauns in the park, some trees may fall. But not tonight.

Dem Bones

Her colleagues said Ruth would be late for her own funeral. Well, she was late for her mother's. She had just been so busy that morning at the old house, trying to finish sorting through her mother's belongings, to get the place ready for the realtor's team, who would prepare it to go on the market in time for house-buying season. She had meant to get to the church early, to meet the minister and make sure of the program. Even after two decades of college teaching, she didn't like speaking impromptu. But all week long, as she went through the house, she had put off the composition of the eulogy.

And now here she was, on a bright afternoon in late February, rushing into the big suburban church, where she was greeted by a friend of her mother's and directed to the front pew. As soon as she sat down, the minister, in a blinding white robe, gestured to her as the next speaker.

She made her way past the gleaming casket at the

foot of the sanctuary, wishing she had worn something more elegant than a dark pants suit and flats. But this was about as elegant as her wardrobe got.

She stepped up to the lectern and looked out over the big white barn of a church. The minister sat a few feet away, behind a low wooden wall, in profile to the congregation. And the "congregation" filled just three pews. Then row upon row of empty blond wood. There was Ruth's father, who had driven from the city. Beside him sat her daughter Harper, yellow hair shining against a black dress. There was a pew full of her mother's friends, beauty-parlored older ladies whom Ruth had met earlier that week, all of them parishioners of this church. In the aisle, seated in a wheelchair, there was Essie, who had worked as the family's maid for many years, wearing a dark beret above her close-cropped silver hair. In the pew beside her was the only other dark face in the room, belonging to her son John.

Ruth looked for a moment out the tall windows. A shoal of birds rose and whirled, calling to each other. Something calmed her. She gripped the lectern with both hands. And then she spoke.

"I didn't know my mother well. I haven't seen her in I don't know how many years. Eight? Nine?" She looked at her father, his gray head tilted like a schooner in the wind. He nodded slightly. "Until I cleaned up the house this week, I didn't know that she had gotten into painting. I didn't know she had made these lovely friends. I didn't know that she had turned to Christianity. How weird is that?"

Beside her, the minister shook her shiny shoulder-length brown hair. "I mean," Ruth added, "how weird is it that I didn't know? I don't know what she had for breakfast—but if her pantry is any evidence, I'm guessing Special K." A couple of the ladies smiled. "I don't know what it was like for her to live alone. Or what she thought about when she lay awake at night. Did she worry that she had driven her husband away?" Ruth's father frowned—or maybe that was just his usual look of consternation. "Was she disappointed that her only child didn't stay in touch? Maybe she lay there thinking about her next painting. I don't know.

"If you're wondering, 'Why is this woman speaking?'—well, I've been wondering the same thing. I hope I'll learn some things from other speakers. But I did live with Twyla Robinson Simon for eighteen years. I am her only child. And I've just spent a week in her house. Here's what I think I know."

All the eyes were on her. It was like leading a class, when it's going well.

"She was kind. She never raised her voice at me. Well, OK, maybe once—but I deserved it." The ladies smiled.

"She was generous. She drove me to piano lessons and dance classes and swim team practices, and never complained. I wish I could say that I still play piano or dance or swim. But that wasn't the point.

"She was lonely. But who isn't?" Essie seemed to nod a little. "When she took her nightly bath, she wanted me to be there, just to keep her company. I don't know what we said. Probably nothing profound. But she wanted me to be part of that ritual. I'll never forget it.

"I think she got herself into a life she wasn't quite prepared for." Ruth looked at her father, who held her gaze. "I don't think that was anybody's fault. I mean, how can you prepare for all the strangeness of life? If you were prepared for everything, you'd never grow. What if you build a life with one person, but you and that person grow apart? What if you give birth to someone, and that person leaves? What prepares you for that?"

The whole pew of older ladies was nodding now. "If you're Twyla Simon, you don't complain. You cut your losses. You welcome others into your life."

Ruth paused, and looked out the nearest window.

"I wish she had recycled." She gazed at the coffin. "Really, Mom. It's not that hard!" Looking back at the pews, she said, "I teach Environmental Studies, I can't help it. But there are probably things my daughter wishes I would do, too."

Harper nodded. The ladies smiled.

"I'm sure some of you know there's a theory called the Gaia hypothesis. It was first proposed in the seventies. Gaia is the whole planet personified, the planet as one organism in which every part relates to every other part, the same way your lungs and your kidneys and your toes are part of one creature. This theory enjoyed a little flurry of interest, and then, in the eighties, it was dismissed as just a wishful myth—some loose, unscientific talk about The Great Earth Mother. You could hear the serious academics scoff.

"Well, thirty years later, that theory is coming back. It's not just loose talk. We know, for instance, that oxygen emitted by the Amazon rainforest sweeps north and condenses over the Arctic, helping maintain some of the dwindling ice cap. Ten thousand miles away. We know that as the ice cap melts, coastal sea level rises in Miami. Ten thousand miles away. How does the old song go? De hip bone connected to de thigh bone, de thigh bone connected to de knee bone, de knee bone connected to de shin bone, now hear the word of the Lord."

Essie looked ready to sing along.

"I'm not saying that Twyla Simon was The Great Earth Mother. In fact, I think she was pretty clueless about being a mother at all. I don't think it was her calling, whatever 'calling' is. I think she did it because it was expected at the time, and she didn't know what else to do, and expectations are a powerful force. I don't know what her real calling would have been. Maybe it was painting. Maybe it was being part of the Ladies Auxiliary in this church. Maybe she never found it. She wouldn't be the first. But we were connected, my mother and I, like a hip bone and a thigh bone, like the Amazon and the Arctic, for better and for worse. I think she did the best she knew how. Angels can do no more."

Ruth paused. How long had she been up here? How much did they want? She knew that the cardinal sin of public speaking is going on too long. Leave them wanting more. And yet she had more to say.

"About the Christian thing." She felt her chest tighten, like a bud before opening.

"I'm not a theologian. I was brought up as a secular Jew, and I never really knew the Jewish principles, let alone the Christian ones. I thought it was a lot of mumbo-jumbo. Ancient texts, don't eat shellfish on Tuesdays, don't have sex with people who have the same genitals you have. Talk about unscientific. When I heard that my mother had become part of this church, I thought she had just traded one brand of mumbo-jumbo for another."

She looked at the minister, who was gazing into her own lap. The part in her hair was impeccable.

"But the Christian jumbo includes the resurrection of Jesus. Growing up, I thought this was crazy. The disciples must have been smoking some loco weed. The writers of the gospels just couldn't resist a good wacky story. It's classic wish-fulfillment. Remember the Roadrunner cartoons?"

She got a big smile from John, Essie's son. OK. Even if he was the only one who got it, that was enough for her.

"I loved those cartoons. They were all about Wile E. Coyote trying to catch the Roadrunner. He set elaborate traps, all of which came from the Acme Company. There was dynamite that the Roadrunner was supposed to set off, but it always blew up in Wile E.'s face; there were guillotines that were supposed to chop off the Roadrunner's head but wound up slicing Wile E. in two; there was an ingenious roadside attraction that would lure the Roadrunner off a cliff, but he was so fast he just zipped right across to the other side, and when Wile E. followed, his legs pumping wildly in mid-air, he plummeted, and after a long second there would be a tiny puff of dust at the bottom of the cliff. The Roadrunner was always too quick for him. " She was tempted to say "Meep! Meep!"—but this didn't seem like the right occasion. Let John imagine it for himself. "Poor Mister Coyote always took some version of that fatal dive. And yet—this is the beauty part—somehow, after the tiny puff of dust, there he was again in the next scene, hale and hearty, working on the next infallible contraption for terminating that damn Roadrunner.

"You know, it *is* crazy. It's cartoon wish-fulfillment. As Jim Morrison said, no one here gets out alive. He sure didn't."

What was she talking about? Maybe she had spent too much time alone this week. Well, what the hell. She looked at the coffin and went on.

"My mother went off the cliff. I don't think she's coming back."

Ruth let this sentence hang. Out the window, everything was still.

"But she's also still alive." Ruth looked at Harper. "She's in her granddaughter, of whom she would be very proud." She looked at the pew full of ladies. "She's in her lovely friends, who welcomed me into their circle earlier this week. She's in that old house, that's for damn sure. Does anyone here need a vanity table?" No one stirred. "She's in me, whether I like it or not. I might as well like it. I've decided that in the next life, she's going to be a devoted recycler."

And then the tears came. Ruth didn't fight them. She just stopped talking. When she stepped down from the sanctuary, she laid a hand on the coffin. And then she sat down.

On the drive back to Vermont the next day, she and Harper were largely silent. Somewhere around Schenectady, Harper said, "Dad's back."

Six years before, he had cleared out, just like the kind of husband and father he never intended to be. Intentions are matchsticks. When Mac left, Ruth had already survived a bout with cancer; she was back at work, teaching and mobilizing environmentalist efforts in Burlington. Harper was thirteen—old enough, he thought, for him to get out of the way. He knew it was unconscionable. But it was his only life. He would do it again.

He had wandered for those six years—north, mostly, up the Connecticut River, through the Northeast Kingdom, into Quebec and back again. He stopped in small towns and worked when he needed the money. He was healthy and able-bodied. He had never needed glasses. After fifteen years as a reference librarian, he was done with the nine-to-five. He worked as a handyman, a bouncer, a gardener. He did a stint at a doggy day care. On a good night at a casino in Montreal, he could make enough at Texas Hold'em to cover food for weeks. Sometimes he slept in his truck. On an empty two-lane blacktop near Lunenburg, he saw the northern lights, great dancing streams of gold and green. Some nights he spent in the homes of women who were as eager for company as he was. One such interlude lasted more than six months, until she started talking about the future. He didn't mean to be cruel. It would be cruel to stay on false pretenses. He left that night.

He drifted back to Burlington. He knew he had no right to return to his old home on Louise Street—and he didn't. The city was just big enough that you could go your own way, if you kept your head down. He slept on an old friend's couch in the Old North End and steered clear of the parts of town that belonged to his wife. He walked and wondered and picked up litter. He drank some beers. The old friend told him that Harper worked at Pho Hong, just down the street. One day, Mac surprised her in a bakery called Knead. She was a tall young woman with long yellow hair. She said, "You have to leave."

He tried. He drove down to the place where he grew up, the old farmhouse in Addison County, where his older brother invited him to stay and help run the farm. He tried, and he couldn't stand it. He knew his sister-in-law didn't want him there. He didn't blame her. He had built a life on leaving that place. He left again. It was Louise Street or nothing.

Ruth took him in—with conditions. He would sleep on the sofa in the study. She was back in chemo, used to having her own bedroom, managing the nausea by staying busy on campus and in town. He would sell his old gas-hog truck. His truck! He couldn't stand it. But he was almost out of m-m-money. He could walk. He would abide by the hours of the house. It sounded like a convent. But since Harper worked late at Pho Hong and Ruth was always up early, the hours seemed elastic. Mother and daughter rarely dined together. They shared the Subaru. It would be like college kids sharing a house off-campus. He said OK.

April morphed into May. The days grew warmer, the nights stayed cool. At breakfast one day, Ruth announced the next crazy decision. Mac made an effort to be there at breakfast, even though he never wanted to eat anything that early. Harper was still in bed. He made a pot of coffee and drank it down mug after mug. Ruth wasn't doing coffee now. She was at the table, reviewing notes for class.

"I'm meeting with a lawyer today," she said.

"What about?"

"I'm giving my mother's house to Essie."

"What?"

"My mother's house. In New Jersey."

He had visited the house in the early years of their marriage, when her parents were still together. It was a big old place in a decent suburb not far from the city. Three bedrooms. A yard. A well-respected school district.

"But it must be worth a million dollars. More."

"Probably."

"Is that fair to Harper?"

"Harper is fine with it."

"Yeah, but—she's nineteen. She doesn't know any-thing about money."

"Maybe that's a good thing," said Ruth.

He took a long sip of coffee.

"Have you talked to Essie?" He had never met her, but he knew what long service she had done in that house.

"Not yet. I'm going to ask the lawyer to work it out with her son John."

"Are you sure they'll be interested?"

"I'm not sure about anything." She gathered papers into her canvas book bag. "Why wouldn't they be interested? It's a nice house."

"Yeah, but—it's a completely white neighborhood. Do you think they'd be comfortable?"

She gave him a steady look. "If they're not, they can sell it, right?"

He drove her to campus. She wanted to take the bus, but if he drove her, she could preserve strength for the day's work. As they pulled up in front of her building, he asked, "Is this a guilt thing?"

"Is what a guilt thing?"

"The house. Essie."

She said, "It's a justice thing."

When she used words like "justice," he didn't know what to say. It felt like any step could hit a landmine. She got out of the car and leaned in the passenger-side window. "Thanks for the ride. Don't wait dinner for me. I've got a meeting in town."

She hadn't given him a house key yet. Maybe that was an oversight. Maybe he had to ask. There was a key on the keychain hanging from the ignition. And there was a locksmith on North Street who would make him a copy for two bucks. But he didn't take it there.

He didn't mind sleeping in the study. It was good to be on the ground floor, with his wife and daughter moving above and around him. He could sleep anywhere. With a pillow and a blanket for these cold May nights—Ruth turned the furnace way down overnight—the couch was as cushy as a sleigh bed.

But he had strange dreams. He was lying in bed with Monday, the family cat of his childhood. She was a brown tiger with a white streak above her golden eyes. They had found her in the barn, ragged, feral, afraid of everything. At age twelve, he had been the one to nurse her back to health with an eyedropper full of milk that he trained her to accept. He spent hours on the kitchen floor, coaxing her to come out from behind the wood-stove. She responded to no one but him. Now, in his dream, Monday was the size of a human being, lying with him, welcoming his caresses with a rumbling purr. And then the cat became human, female, purring still. She didn't have a face, but even in the dream he knew that she was far too young for him. Well, he couldn't be responsible for his dreams.

When he got back to Louise Street, he set the keys on the kitchen counter. Force of habit. And it wasn't his car. Upstairs, he heard music from Harper's room. Reggae today. She never seemed to listen to the same genre two days in a row. For the first time since his return, he knocked at her door.

She opened it, barefoot, in flannel pajama bottoms and a shapeless dark-blue Smith sweatshirt that had belonged to her grandmother. Her uneven yellow hair draped over her shoulders. At six foot three, Mac was used to gazing down at people. Not Harper. Her eyes were almost level with his. Behind her, the ceiling was still as they had painted it together ten years before: midnight blue with constellations of their own invention. Cap'n Crunch. The Wheelbarrow. Harold brandishing his crayon.

"I brung you a sneck-lifter," he said.

She waited for him to explain.

"Sneck," he said, "is a Scottish word for a latch. A sneck-lifter is the item you take to someone's house — the bottle of wine, the bibelot — to encourage your host to lift the latch for you."

"Cool," she said.

He pulled something from his hip pocket and said, "Voilà." It was a Pez dispenser — the Little Mermaid edition. That had been her favorite story when she was a child. He pressed the tab at the back of Ariel's head, and she disgorged a purplish brick of candy that clashed with her flaming plastic hair. "Fully loaded!" he said, handing it to his daughter. "I won't tell your mother about the candy."

She accepted it and said, "Thanks." Then she fished her phone from a deep pajama pocket and checked the time. "I gotta get dressed," she said. She was taking a class at the community college, working on her GED.

Then she would report for her dinner shift at Pho Hong. He nodded, and she shut the door.

Many rivers to cross. He was going to need pontoons.

Harper took the car, and the house was suddenly empty. His heart thrummed with caffeine. It was a bright afternoon. He took a walk.

His eyes teared up immediately. He could practically see the pollen in the golden haze. How could something as lovely as apple blossoms be so noxious?

Pine Street was busier than ever. Here was a fancy new wine bar—new, at least, to him. From the window he could see high tables and heavy hanging lamps. Further up the street, he lingered outside a place devoted to cider. Inside, it was all shining surfaces, flooded with sunlight. Where were the dark, fusty bars of the past? The Sheik? The Chickenbone? What if you just wanted a Bud? You were in the wrong town.

At the foot of Maple, he found that the bike path was closed. Lake Champlain was at flood stage, thanks to snow melt and spring rains. And maybe climate change, too? Ruth would know. The flood was not a rolling tide, like a river in spate. It was just standing water, a platinum sheet stretching ten miles to the Adirondacks. Perkins Pier was under water. The tops of picnic tables protruded like rafts. There were twenty-two candidates for the Democratic presidential nomination. What were they going to do about this?

The boardwalk was almost empty. A couple of joggers, a woman walking four dogs. He hoped she was well provided with plastic bags. Where was everyone? Did they all have jobs except him?

He labored back up the hill. When did Depot Street become so steep? At the top, he emerged in the Old North End. Here, surely, there would be a real bar.

The Lamplighter was a little too cute—micro-brews, small plates: when did everything go miniature? —but they had a fine selection of middle-American beers. He got a Schlitz and pressed the bottle to his cheek. Even on a cool day, this was how you drink a beer.

There was a *Burlington Free Press* on the bar. He remembered when it had been something like a real newspaper, laid out horizontally, with substantial sections and local columnists. Now it was a tabloid wrapper for a *USA Today* insert. But it still had baseball scores. The Red Sox had lost again.

Hours later, he walked out into the late spring night. The air was rich with toxins. He pulled up his collar and cried.

That night, when Harper logs into her mother's laptop, she doesn't mean to snoop. But she can't help noticing its recent browsing history.

Baseball, baseball, baseball. How can someone care so much about men hitting balls with sticks? Or, more often, missing balls with sticks? It's one of the world's great mysteries.

Classic British sports cars. Sleek Aston Martins in colors like pewter and onyx. Do they all have ejector seats?

Real estate listings. Penthouse apartments in the massive new development in Winooski, looking out over the river; condos in Burlington citadels, gazing across the lake. What is the thing about views of water? And didn't he just move back in? Well, everyone's entitled to their dreams.

After a full night shift at Pho Hong, she can't concentrate on her online reading for Bio. Somewhere beyond the kitchen window, a dog is barking ceaselessly. Harper gets up. Maybe she can do this in the morning.

It's her job to lock up the house before going to bed. Down the hall, the door to the study is standing open, and the room is dark. She steps in without switching on a light, and confirms that the couch is empty. The old horsehair blanket lies in a heap. Standing in the dark, she folds it neatly. Then she picks up the pillow, too.

She carries this armload upstairs, to a door at the end of the hall. On the rear of the house is a narrow porch that looks over their small back yard. Through the long months of cold, it gets no use.

She opens the door and steps outside. There's a small table with two straight-back chairs; there's a collection of clay pots in many sizes, waiting for summer bulbs. And there's the old day-bed—an iron frame with a squeaking metal lattice supporting a thin mattress, comfortable only to the desperate or the oblivious. As a child, at her father's suggestion, she sometimes slept out here on hot summer nights. Her mother didn't believe in air conditioning. During her renegade years, after sneaking out, she sometimes made her way back home this way. If you were careful—and not too heavy—you could climb the trellis on the side of the house and pull yourself right up to the porch, where you could flake out on the day-bed. One morning earlier this week, she had seen the outline of a lanky body underneath that thin bedspread.

She sets down the pillow and spreads out the blanket, then sits on the edge of the bed. The dog has stopped barking. Faint sounds of traffic wash up from Pine Street. In a bedroom beyond the fence, a light winks out. Above the dark maples, there's a bright fingernail of waning moon. The night smells of damp earth, waiting. She shivers, and is tempted to crawl under the covers. Just for now.

She rises, smooths the blanket, and steps inside. And then she turns the lock.

A Person Goes Out on the Town

His first love was baseball. The 1978 Boston Red Sox, to be exact—one must be exact about love. Luis Tiant, Rick Burleson, Jerry Remy, Carlton Fisk, Bob Stanley, Jim Rice, Fred Lynn, and Carl Yastrzemski at the end of his great career, hobbling to the plate, his legs more bandaged every week. How could they not win it all for Yaz?

Eustace McKenzie, better known as Mac, was eight years old that summer, just beginning to learn what love can be. He followed the Sox as closely as they could be followed, pre-Internet, from a farm in Addison County, Vermont. He had never been to Fenway Park. His father said they couldn't make such a trip in growing season—and baseball season was growing season, from planting to harvest. Mac whined—but briefly, as he knew it would do no good. They were pinned to their two hundred acres. He had to live with the Fenway he saw in his mind—the impossibly green field, lit up against the city night; the severe and beautiful geometry of its dimensions, from

Pesky's Pole in right field to the Triangle in deep right center to The Green Monster in left, looming so close to the plate. Yaz might not be fast anymore, but he knew how to play every inch of that wall.

Night after night, Mac saw it all on the radio. He wasn't allowed to watch TV on worknights, and virtually every night was a worknight on the farm. But he could listen after Lights Out, with the sound turned down low so as not to trouble his brother, who slept across the room. At ten, Tom said he was too old for baseball. He was reading comic books, or writing notes to Stacey Johnson in his class, listening to pop music on his own radio. Mac didn't think it was a question of age. Mr. Pijinowski, the crossing guard, was in his seventies, and he was the biggest Red Sox fan in town. Mac didn't care what Tom thought.

Their mother always came in to check on them before she went to bed. When she found that the radio was still murmuring low by Mac's bed, she switched it off. Sometimes he heard that click and didn't move because he was tired, it was late, he was supposed to be asleep. He would get the score from the sports news in the morning.

Now, in the summer of 2019, he is forty-eight, and he knows how silly it all is. When he runs into Silverman, his old pal from the library, he focuses first on politics—all those Democratic candidates. Can anyone beat Trump? But sooner or later the talk comes around to the Sox. Silverman thinks the manager has lost control of the team after their big success last season. Mac says, "Well, you know what they say about managers. They're smart enough to understand the game, but stupid enough to think it's important."

Silverman laughs. And then they talk about tonight's pitching matchup against the Twins.

It would be easier to keep up if he still had a job at the university library, where he could check scores and analysis between encounters at the reference disk. But he had quit that job cold when he left town six years ago. It would be easier if he had a smartphone, or a laptop of his own. But on that rainy October morning when he left his wife and daughter, he chucked his cellphone into the woods behind their little house. He cut his credit cards in two. All he took with him was his old green pickup and the family dog, which would be dead within months. He was going north. He didn't want to keep up with the world. Let the world try to keep up with him.

Now he's back, tail tucked between his legs. Six years of North made him nothing but older. He's worn the faces off all the cards. Amazingly, his wife has taken him back in—to sleep on the fold-out couch in the study. Ruth is somewhere in the limbo of breast cancer; she gets her treatments and doesn't talk about it. She is more engaged than ever in environmental activism. Their daughter Harper, at 19, is waiting tables and taking classes for her GED at the community college. They share the Subaru. Mac thought his return would be a big deal; he thought he would have to justify him-self, eat crow, make good. But his wife and daughter have hardly broken stride. When they are both out of the house, he logs onto Ruth's laptop and catches up on mlb.com.

Aside from that, he walks. He doesn't have a job yet. After years of freelancing, doing odd jobs to cover expenses, it ought to feel familiar; it ought to feel fine. But being back in Burlington, where he worked for years with benefits and a pension, makes it feel like playing hooky. His overhead is low. He doesn't even have the upkeep of the old truck, which Ruth made him sell as a quid pro quo for moving back in. She said it was an environmental nightmare, and he didn't doubt her sincerity—but he can't help feeling that she also wanted to make it harder for him to cut and run again.

So he walks instead, and he winds up in bars where he can catch up on the Sox in a discarded newspaper, maybe chat with a friendly barkeep. The guy at The Lamplighter, up on North Ave., is a Yankees fan, which is usually the kiss of death—they're so smug. But Boyd is old enough to remember what happened in 1978, and to show some sympathy for a fan dying hard. In July of that season, the Sox had a fourteen-game lead. By the end of September, the Yankees had caught them, forcing a one-game playoff for the pennant. It was played at Fenway. It did not go well. Eight-year-old Mac was disconsolate for weeks. Now, in another bright New England June, the Sox are deep in third place, and so he sits at The Lamplighter, where Boyd torments him with tales of the Yankee miracle of '78. Mac doesn't believe in miracles. He believes in taking a strike and hitting the cutoff man.

And then he steps out, to walk back through town toward his wife's home in the South End. Not his home, although it once was. At eight o'clock, it's the magic hour in Burlington—sun setting on the lake, young couples strolling Church Street, outdoor tables filled with raucous diners, money spilling out of their pockets. Mac has fifty-five dollars to his name, and he is a little drunk. A busker juggles fire for a large, admiring crowd. He shouts, "I see there aren't any dark-skinned people in the crowd. What happened to all the melanin in this town?" They're hip enough to know that they're supposed to laugh.

Mac's stomach is growling; beer nuts may not be enough to keep a lanky man alive. Do they still have gravy fries at Nectar's?

They do. And they're still ridiculously delicious, hot and salty, glutinously filling. On a low stage at the back of the long narrow room, a local band is playing, loud. Above the bar, several large screens show the Red Sox just getting underway out in Minnesota. This is one of those places, Mac thinks, that doesn't know what it is: Low-rent restaurant? Sports bar? Music venue? Hipster hangout? A little bit of everything for middle-of-the-roaders like him? He doesn't care. The fries are hot, and the beer is cold. The Sox might get it going on this road trip. What's fifty dollars for? But he can't ignore the band. For just three guys—guitar, drums, and bass—they generate a hellacious noise. Mac remembers how Springsteen described the mission of his early bar bands: "Get up there, plug in, and *detonate*." These guys are exploding. The drummer hits the snare as if it stole his girlfriend. It rackets like a belt buckle left in the dryer. The guitarist wheels his free arm like Pete Townshend, one two power shift. The bassman drives a single groove, *doobita doobita doobita*. It's all a little drunk.

And then, of a sudden, the bass and the drums drop out, and it's just a lonesome-road guitar, and Mac actually recognizes a song: "Oh, Mary, Don't You Weep." The guy intones it in a street-church sigh that would make Aretha proud. Mac checks the laminated calendar on the bar, and sees that these guys are called The Darling Buds.

At least, he thinks they're guys. The guitarist appears to be wearing a skirt. But it's a warm night. It works in Scotland.

When the bass and the drums start flailing again, Mac turns his attention back to the ballgame. The Sox are already trailing, 3-0.

On his way back from the bathroom, he notices that there's another middle-aged guy sitting alone, at a table by the open front window, as far from the band as possible. The man looks familiar—closely cropped graying hair, square jaw, big gut held in by a blue button-down. He is nursing a tall glass of something clear, with a wedge of lime. And he is gazing intently at the band.

Mac looks again at The Darling Buds, and then he twigs. The guitarist—the guy in the skirt—it's Josh, who has been a friend of Harper's for years. And the blue-collar Buddha in the window seat—that's Josh's father, who works as a foreman for a big Burlington construction company. Years ago, when Mac took Harper to the skate park on the waterfront, he would often see Josh, always in a black t-shirt, shoulder-length dark hair flying as he ruled the big bowl. And he sometimes saw Josh's father arrive in a big company truck to pick him up. Josh was never happy to see him. They lived in an apartment complex just down the hill from Mac and Ruth's tidy neighborhood. Mac didn't know what had become of Josh's mother.

He picks up his latest beer and heads over to the man's little table. The Sox are in the dumpster. The band is crazy loud. It's bachelor's night out. What does he have to lose?

When he gestures inquiringly at the chair next to Josh's father, Josh's father nods. The band sounds a little better from here, with an irregular wash of street traffic and sidewalk talk just out the window. After a few minutes, they take a break.

In the sudden quiet, Mac says, "That's your boy, isn't it?"

The man nods, and takes a sip from his glass.

"Josh, right?"

"Josh was their deadname."

"What?"

"They go by River now."

Harper has told him about this. Josh, with whom she spends a lot of time, has started using they/them pronouns. She didn't mention the name thing. River? Really?

"How can you stand it?" he says. He can't help himself.

The man gazes at him, hard. Plates clink in the kitchen.

"I mean," Mac says, "doesn't it bother you?"

The man shakes his head, and takes another slow sip.

"It would bother me," Mac says. "My daughter goes out with your son—I mean, they hang out together, I don't know what the hell kids do these days, do they still have boyfriends and girlfriends? They don't seem to have dates. We used to go to dinner or a movie, you know?" He remembers getting up the nerve to ask Jill Gustafson out in eighth grade—planning the dinner at Cubber's, the walk to the gazebo, the hoped-for goodnight kiss. "I'm Mac, by the way."

The man shakes the proffered hand and says, "Ted."

"So," Mac says, "Doesn't it bother you? I'm just the father of the girl who's hanging out with him, or them, or whatever, and it bothers *me*."

The man looks at him drily. "Why should it bother you? It's not your life."

"But—it's like a *comment* on my life."

"I don't see it that way," the man says. "But even if I did—who cares if it's a comment on your life? People are full of comments. People can comment all they want. It's a free country. But they can't touch my life."

"So it doesn't bother you."

"Don't make me hit you," says River's father. "I don't want to hit you."

Mac thinks he means it. Part of him wants to find out. But just then the band starts up again, boom-shacka-lacka, and the men turn their attention back to the stage.

Is Josh—River—wearing eye shadow now? And dark lipstick? The band sounds even drunker. Maybe that's a good thing.

Mac goes back to the bar for another beer. Up on the screen, he sees that the Sox are up 5-4 in the seventh. What do you know.

Earlier that evening, he had stopped in at Pho Hong. It was early in Harper's dinner shift; the place was mostly empty. He didn't want food yet, and he didn't care much for their low-rent noodles, anyway. They didn't have a liquor license; they were strictly BYOB. This always seemed like a mistake to him. What if you just wanted to hang out for a while? What if the tables were all busy but you wanted to wait? You had to sit on this hard little bench by the entrance and listen to exasperated would-be diners deciding where to go instead. But he was just here to say hi.

Harper was shuttling briskly back and forth from the kitchen to the two tables already occupied. She nodded to him and continued about her business. Mac was still getting used to the idea of his daughter as a grown-up in the world — this tall young woman, long blond hair trailing over a black Pho Hong t-shirt almost to the waist of her jeans, bustling about so capably. Six years ago, she was still The Bean, anxious about shadows in her bedroom.

If you were to judge his action solely by this result, you couldn't say he had done the wrong thing. She had been too dependent, clinging to her father. He left. She grew up into this brisk young woman who was waiting on that four-top with easy grace. She was taking the bus every day over to the community college for those hard science classes. She was taking care of her mother through treatments for cancer. She was making a life in the world. You couldn't say he'd been wrong.

When she seemed to have a moment between orders, he went over to the counter where she stood to look out for new arrivals and to answer the phone about take-out. She said, "Hi, Dad."

"Hey, kid." He picked up a cellophane-wrapped peppermint.

"What's up?" She looked down at a list of some kind.

"Nothing. Just thought I'd stop by."

"Sorry I don't have time to talk."

"You guys should put in a bar."

"Yeah, that's what some people say." She looked over at her two tables.

"That way, a person would have a place to hang out." He had always referred to himself as "a person." She used to say, "You mean *you*!" Now she just nodded.

"Besides, a person likes a nice upholstered stool. Always better than a hard wooden bench."

The phone rang, and she took an order. "Thirty-five minutes," she said.

When she put the phone down, he said, "That's a long wait. You guys aren't that busy."

"There's only one guy in the kitchen."

"Oh." He fingered the peppermint, still in its wrapper. "You think they could use some help?"

She looked at him.

"For real," he said. "A person used to do a mean stir-fry, you know."

She said, "This is real Vietnamese cooking. Done by real Vietnamese people. That's the whole point."

OK, maybe she wasn't so grown-up. She still had that thirteen-year-old righteousness. He peeled the wrapper from the candy and popped it into his mouth.

"Sounds like discrimination to me," he said. "Who says a white guy from Addison County can't do Vietnamese? I can do Cheerios, I can do cinnamon toast, I can do eggs any style. Over easy, over hard, yolk broke, you name it."

She looked up from her list. "Stop it, Dad."

"Stop what?" '

"Stop flirting with me."

"What?"

"I'm at *work*," she said. "I gotta take care of those tables."

"So take care of them. Don't let your father get in your way."

She took a pad and pencil from her apron, and stuck the pencil in the hair behind her ear. It was heartbreaking.

"I was not flirting," he added. "Believe me, if I had been flirting, you'd know it."

"Whatever," she said, and headed over to one of her tables, all smiling business.

He put the candy wrapper down on the counter. Where could he go? Somewhere. Outside.

Outside, it was a bright June evening.

And now he's headed home from Nectar's, belly full of gravy fries and beer. The Sox have a late-inning lead.

Nobody hit him. The Darling Buds got drunker. Pharaoh's army got drownded.

Crickets are singing, and fireflies wink in the shrubs along South Winooski Avenue. Hardly a car in sight. He's walking home. Well, OK, "home,"

When he gets there, of course, the doors are locked. It's after midnight. Ruth has been in bed for hours. Harper—who knows where Harper is. She's a grown-up now, righteousness and all. The doors are locked, the doors are locked.

But there's the trellis on the side of the house, which a person can climb to the back porch, where there's a comfy day-bed. Well, not so comfy really—the metal frame creaks and the mattress is thin—but at this time of night, a bed is a bed.

He starts climbing. Sneakers would be better than these work boots. But sneakers aren't his look. This used to be easier. Somebody has let the vines grow out too much; it's hard to get his fingers through to the wood. He slips and falls.

Good thing it's grass down here. Still, his back hurts. Hurts hurts hurts. When he opens his eyes, he can't see any stars. Must be a cloudy night. His mother used to tell him that even when it's cloudy, even in the daylight, the stars are always out there. He can feel the earth whirling, *doobita doobita doobita.* He gets up, and climbs again. This time, he pulls himself right onto the porch, the champion of all trellis-climbers. Here is the day bed. Someone has put out a blanket and pillow. There is a God. His back feels fine. He drifts off to sleep, hoping that the bullpen holds on.

ANDANTE

She comes to him.

He wakes to a soft touch across his brow, and wonders if it's part of a dream. He keeps his eyes closed. Fingers rove over his cheek, his slightly crooked nose, over his lips and chin. Slowly, they trace the underside of his jaw. Once she had kissed him there, under his jaw, on a smoky August afternoon in Paris, as they stood on the worn floorboards of a café neither of them would ever see again.

The hand descends, to his chest, his belly. He opens his eyes, and then his mouth—but before he can speak, she shakes her head. Hush, she doesn't say. Hush.

She is lying beside him on the fold-out sofa, where he has slept since he moved back in. Their nineteen-year-old daughter could be sleeping upstairs. He can't keep track of her, and knows he shouldn't try. Most nights, his wife also sleeps upstairs. Because of her treatments, she goes to bed early. He tries to stay out of the way. Sometimes he drinks too much. Sometimes, when the doors are locked, he sleeps on the back porch. But tonight he's on the sofa, in the study, and now here she is, in the dim light from a streetlamp that slants through the blinds. It's July, and the windows are open. Louise Street is quiet. She is small as she always was. Her dark frizzy hair, which has fallen out and grown again, tickles just below his chin.

He unbuttons and pulls off her blouse. When he looks at the scars on her chest, she winces but she doesn't quail. She buries her head in his armpit. He can hear her twenty-five years ago, saying she loved his farmboy smell. Soon, all their clothes are cast aside, and she is on top of him. He hardly knows what is happening. He proceeds haltingly, not wanting to hurt her more than he already has.

At some point, he thinks he hears the kitchen door, and footsteps in the hall, then on the stairs. But they are making noises of their own, and the world beyond the study door is furlongs and fathoms away.

In the silence that follows, her voice is soft and low.

Tell me a badtime story.

He used to tell stories to their daughter when she couldn't sleep. But what can he tell now?

Tell about the Hotel du Paradis, she says.

The Hotel—?

Du Paradis. In Paris.

Oh, he says. On that little square in Montmartre.

She nods.

How many stars did we give it?

A dozen. A hundred. A sky full.

Do I have to say Hotel with the hat over the o?

Yes. Right is right.

He remembers the Hôtel du Paradis. They never stayed there, never even went inside. On their one trip to Paris, twenty years ago, they stayed in a place that belonged to a family she knew from her year of study abroad—a fifth-floor walk-up with a bathroom down the hall. It was summer, and hot, with no air conditioning; they kept the one window open, and traffic noise drifted up from the rue du Faubourg Poissonnière. In the daylight, they made the short walk to Montmartre, and happened on a slanting, cobbled plaza with a single bench and a spreading plane tree. The Place Emile Goudeau. One side of the square was a wall of whitewashed stucco with green awnings above all the windows. They sat on the bench and watched the guests come and go.

You know, he says, they say Picasso used to hang out there with Max Jacob.

She nods.

But I don't think it's true, he says. It would have been too posh for them. It was really something in those days— up on top of Paris, when no one had a telephone and the windmills were still turning on the hill. Sometimes it took days for the news to arrive from the city. At the Hôtel du Paradis, they didn't care.

They didn't care, she murmurs. They didn't care.

A car sweeps by outside.

At the Hôtel du Paradis, he says, there was a boy from the provinces who worked as a *garçon de service*.

What did he do?

Whatever they needed. He washed dishes. He carried suitcases. He hauled dirty linens to the Bateau Lavoir, where they got the laundry done. The laundry girls splashed him playfully. He loved that, for reasons they would never know. He was too young to wait on tables, but sometimes, in a pinch, they dressed him in black trousers and a white shirt, and he did that, too. He was tall for his age.

It was a good life for a boy who had run away from home in Angoulème. He didn't want to be a farmer like his father and his brother. He lived on the roof of Paris. Sometimes he snuck into the cabarets on the Place Pigalle. He had a little room on the top floor, under the eaves, among the chambermaids. But he was terrified of them.

Why?

Because . . . he had a secret. He was afraid, they would discover that . . . he was actually a frog.

Really?

Really.

This sounds a little desperate.

But it's true. He had learned to stand on his hind legs; he had trained himself not to croak; but still he was a frog through and through. Sometimes, in spite of his efforts to stay dry, he left a wet trail behind him in the hall.

But?

But what?

There has to be a but. It's not a story yet.

Give me time.

I don't have all night, she says. I have work to do in the morning.

Tomorrow is Sunday.

So?

OK, OK.

She always has work to do in the morning. Even more now that her time is short.

He says, But . . . there was one chambermaid who took an interest in him.

Did she know he was a frog?

She had her doubts. But she didn't care.

She didn't care, she murmurs. She didn't care.

The thing is, he says, this chambermaid had a secret of her own.

What was that?

She was actually a princess.

No.

Yes. She had escaped from the palace, because she didn't want to be a pawn in diplomacy, to marry some prince or dauphin just because her father said so. And also because it was Montmartre, on top of the world. The windmills were turning. So she understood about living in disguise.

Ah. She traces a line down his collarbone. So?

He courted her. He brought her Chinese food.

They had Chinese food then?

They had everything. It was Paris. He walked with her all over the city, up the river and down.

Did he know she was a princess?

He had his doubts. She was full of ideas about making Paris better, cleaner, sweeter for its people. Not many chambermaids think like that. This made him love her even more—and made him even more terrified that she couldn't love him, a mere frog. But still he courted her. He couldn't not love her.

Out the window, some kind of night bird sings.

One day, he says, she got sick.

What made her sick?

She drank too much coffee. Remember when people could drink coffee all day long?

Like Balzac, she says. So?

He took her to the hospital, down in Paris. It had a beautiful name.

Lariboisière.

That's it.

Did she get better?

She got better. He thought they could do anything. He couldn't afford a ring, but he made one out of a sheet of newsprint and surprised her with it at a cafe. She kissed him under the jaw. They married their fortunes together.

He had some real estate there in his bag?

Exactly. Nine months later, she had a beautiful daughter. He was terrified that the daughter would be a frog.

Was she?

She had a greenish tint. But she was OK.

And then?

And then . . . the princess became a queen.

I thought she was living in disguise.

She was, but she couldn't hide her regal qualities. When the old king and queen died, the people needed a new ruler. One day, the chambermaid was walking through the market at Les Halles, and someone shouted, "It's the princess!" Everyone took up the cry, and they hoisted her on their shoulders and called out "Vive la Reine!"

This is a weird story.

You asked for it.

So then what?

The chambermaid became Queen, because she couldn't let the people down, and she had all these ideas to make the city better. And she did. The city gleamed. The people were happy.

But?

Does there have to be a but?

Do you want people to believe this story?

He sighs. In the deep quiet, he hears the ticking of his watch.

But—the *garçon*, who was now Prince Regent, was still a frog. And he hated the palace. It was so dry. When he visited the laundry, the girls froze: what did the Prince Regent want of them? He was tired of standing on his hind legs. He missed the old days, the woods and the weed and the muck. One day, when they were holding court to some fancy foreign delegation, he slipped out the back of the palace, stripped off his culottes, and headed north.

But Angoulême is south.

He didn't want to go where he had been before. He

went north, to Luxembourg and Belgium, to Doggerland and John o' Groats, Lapland and Tasmania.

Tasmania is on the other side of the world.

He got around.

And what did he do all day?

He lived in the muck. He ate a lot of bugs.

I bet he met some more chambermaids.

You don't want to know.

He must have been happy.

Up to a point. This was a frog who had seen Paree.

What about their daughter?

That's the thing that broke his heart. But he knew she would be well tended at the palace.

She doesn't say anything. His watch ticks. He says:

Years passed. He missed his girls. He wanted to know how they were. He went back to Paris.

Mac—

Mac who?

Mac. You know this won't happen again, right?

You don't know that. Did you think it would happen this time?

He starts to sing, in a dusky baritone. "Strange things have happened, like never before . . . ." He doesn't even know what song it is.

Just, she says. Just don't count on it. Don't count on anything.

He pulls the sheet up to their chins. Hush, he doesn't say. Hush.

Then it's Sunday morning in the kitchen. She isn't working. Yet. Summer sunlight is floating in. The radio plays the classical station. He has made coffee; now he is heating the milk.

When their daughter comes in, he's just pouring hot milk into big red bowls full of coffee. The daughter, in gym shorts and a t-shirt, looks a little shook.

Mom, she says, you don't drink coffee!

Her mother raises the bowl to her mouth with both hands and takes a noisy sip.

The daughter stares. The radio announcer says they're broadcasting live from somewhere. Tanglewood? Maybe. They'll be playing arias and barcarolles, everything andante. The oboe gives the orchestra an A.

Toadstools

By midsummer of 2019, City Place Burlington had been a blank expanse of mud and stone for more than a year. At first, the construction site was hard to see, because it was hemmed in by advertisements for the complex under construction: glossy larger-than-life photographs of smiling people engaged in the activities that would occur there. "Live," commanded the caption for one of the pictures, showing a happy couple in their shiny new condo with a view of the lake. "Work," said another, with an image of an immaculate office full of productive employees. The next one said "Shop," and showed two young women sashaying past a streetfront of glitzy stores. "Eat," "Learn," and "Play" were the further imperatives to be accomplished in this paradisaical new development in downtown Burlington, Vermont.

But then Ruth Simon's group, Save Our Spaces, persuaded a court that these sumptuous murals violated the state's law against billboards, and the ads had to come down. They were replaced, immediately, by dull blue wooden panels that simply obscured the view. But if you got close enough to peer through a crack between panels, you could see a city block of sun-smacked rock and dirt pocked with craters where, a year before, excavators had started digging a foundation. Then the developer ran out of money, or ran into legal trouble over permits, or discovered that there weren't actually enough prospective tenants, commercial or residential, to make this thing go forward. Or all of the above. The equipment had simply stopped moving in the summer of 2018, in prime construction weather. Since then, nothing. A few abandoned tractors and backhoes lingered at the edge of a rocky gulch, like jungle animals come to die at a dried-up watering hole. If you gazed up to imagine the twin fourteen-story towers of glass and steel — towers that would be four stories taller than anything else in Burlington, championed by the mayor and supported by public money — all you saw was the high blue sky of mid-July, dusted by smoke from forest fires in central Ontario.

At Ruth Simon's kitchen table on Louise Street, a mile to the south, the opposition lived on. "City Place!" she scoffed. "How generic can you get? It sounds like the marketing people just threw up their hands and went for the default setting. Name it *for* something, or somebody. The Ritz! The Babylon! Mar-a-Lago North!"

One guy at the table said, "Hey. Go easy on our President." Ruth's husband, Mac, who was sitting on a stool at the breakfast bar, didn't know what to make of these guys. He was used to Ruth's projects collecting barnacles of random support, but these guys were different. Mac had seen several of them on benches in City Hall Park, loud and profane, doing nothing, as far as Mac could tell, except scaring people away from the park. But then they had won their way into Ruth's life. In the midst of an action designed to dramatize resistance to the city's plan to renovate that space, Ruth had keeled over in a heap. She was undergoing treatments for breast cancer and trying to keep up her usual work as a teacher and activist; maybe she had pushed herself too hard. Several of these men had helped get her to the hospital that day, then waited until she was cleared at the E. R.

Now here they were, three of them, at the kitchen table while Mac looked on from his stool. One was a tall black guy in a green hoodie, even on this hot July day. One was short and barrel-chested, pumping a foot against the hardwood floor. And one was wearing no shirt, but his torso was all tattoos, from knuckle to earlobe, from waistline to chin, indigo, carmine, viridian. Ruth, whose petite frame was almost lost in this menagerie, sometimes claimed that she was a rabble rouser. Well, Mac thought, she has brought the rabble to her kitchen.

It used to be Mac's kitchen, too, until he lit out on a rainy October morning — out, off, away from his marriage and his thirteen-year-old daughter, away from his job at the university library. He threw his cell phone into the woods and drove his old truck into uncharted territory, out into the thrilling fields of nothing. After six years, he came home. He ate crow. He sold the old truck, and vowed to pitch in. But sometimes his mind still wandered. At the table, they were saying something about mattresses and swimming pools. He decided to cut the grass.

The yard was full of toadstools. They had popped up overnight, white bubbles that littered the grass like tiny space invaders. What was he supposed to do about them? On the farm where Mac grew up, he would have mowed them down without a second thought. They were no earthly good. But what did he know? Maybe they attracted friendly birds that helped pollinate the world. Ruth would know. If those guys weren't in there with her, he would ask. Instead, he steered the mower around them, leaving little almond-shaped islands of long grass, each anchored by a Styrofoam push-pin. It was a look.

When he went back into the kitchen, they were still at the table. What could occupy them so long? There was a little silence.

"You know," he said, standing by the fridge, "the history of that property is really interesting." They all looked up at him. "By the middle of the nineteenth century," he said, "it was a lively neighborhood of wood-frame homes, mostly Italian. A lot of them worked on the waterfront, where tons of timber were shipped every day. There was a thriving Italian market, a bunch of restaurants and cafes, and the biggest Catholic church in Vermont. When my parents came to Burlington from their farm down in Addison County, they always made a special stop for mortadella, and treated themselves to cannoli. By the nineteen-sixties, though, it all seemed too seedy for the powers that be, and they wiped it out, just like that—urban renewal. That's when they put in the mall, and the first of those big ugly block buildings—banks and courthouses and hotels for rich tourists on Battery Street. Did anybody ever like that mall? It was such a crypt—two floors of linoleum and plaster, with the lamest little skylights that just reminded you how dim it was. It's no wonder people voted to get rid of it."

"That's not history," said Ruth. "That's current events." Her pale round face, shaded by dark-framed glasses, was as resolute as ever, even in her sickness. "History," she said, "is the Abenaki people who lived there for thousands of years, hunting and fishing and subsistence farming. History is the valley that was carved by glaciers two hundred million years ago. It's the wetlands that filter our drinking water. It's the seagulls and the lake trout and the worms."

"Right on," said the guy in the tattoo shirt. With his dark slicked-back hair and long sideburns, he looked like Merle Haggard.

"Great," said Mac. "History is the worms." He gestured at the refrigerator. "Didn't I leave some beer in here?"

"You did," said the black guy. "Thanks."

This guy's name, Mac remembered from the day of Ruth's E. R. crisis, was Rowan. He was the guy who always said "Have a great day" as you walked past his bench in the park.

The group at the table apparently had things to do. He decided to head out for his daily walk.

Across the street, he wasn't surprised to see Evie Morrison out in her garden. Evie and Leah had the most gorgeous flowers on the block. She was kneeling by the peonies. She seemed eager to talk.

"When I walked Kinsey this morning," she said, "I was taken aback to see two guys sitting in the chairs on your front lawn." Long ago, Mac and Ruth had put a couple of Adirondack chairs out on the little bluff of patchy grass above the sidewalk.

"Yeah, those chairs almost never get used, do they?" said Mac.

"Who *are* those guys?" said Evie. She wiped her brow with a gloved hand. Her graying shoulder-length hair was held by a single scrunchy in back.

"Just some guys we've gotten to know lately," Mac said. "You know."

"They were smoking," Evie said. "And tossing the butts on the ground."

"Well, tobacco is biodegradable, right?"

"Not the filters," she said.

Mac smiled a rangy smile. Score one for Evie. He didn't know why he took such pleasure in provoking her dudgeon, but it buoyed him every time. She went on.

"Elly Taylor says they're sleeping in your house."

"How would Elly Taylor know? I didn't see her checking beds at Lights Out." He wouldn't put it past her, though. Elly Taylor knew everything about everybody on Louise Street.

"Well, are they?"

"No! That would be crazy! We don't have that many rooms!" As far as Mac knew, he was the only strange homeless man sleeping in the house. "Besides," he said, "Those guys are well-known ne'er-do-wells! Mother-stabbers! Father-rapers! I bet some of them are litterers, too."

Evie sighed. Mac said, "Have a great day," and walked on.

When he got to town, he found City Hall Park was weirdly quiet. He paused by the bench where the homeless guys usually hung out. The city had announced that the park would be renovated this summer — a new fountain, a rain garden, new walkways that would improve drainage, a kiosk for coffee and sandwiches. In preparation for the construction, the farmers' market, a festive event that filled the park every Saturday with white canopies and strolling customers, had been exiled to a parking lot a mile out of town. And then nothing had happened. Here it was mid-July, and the park was as sleepy and scruffy as always. Why the delay? Some bureaucratic boondoggle, no doubt, just another variation on the debacle at City Place. Why couldn't people ever do what they promised to do?

Mac walked on up to The Lamplighter. An old wood-frame storefront bar on North Street, it was just far enough from downtown to be safe from the tourists and the college kids. Mac didn't need twenty local beers on tap. He just wanted a Bud and a cushioned stool in a cool, dark place. Hanging by the bar was a full-size human skeleton, with a placard at the pelvis: "Our Oldest Customer." Affixed to the wall in the alcove by the restrooms, there was a long metal box of the sort that dispenses condoms or tampons, adorned by a cartoon of a buxom, nearly naked woman, with a logo proclaiming "Pecker Stretchers." What the hell was that? Mac didn't want to know.

At the bar, he found himself sitting with a couple of thirty-something guys who worked for S. D. Ireland, the biggest construction company in town. These guys were pissed, in both the British and the American senses. They were supposed to be working on City Place. It was such a huge project, it would have kept them busy for months, if not years.

One of them said to Mac, "We voted for that monstrosity in November of 2016."

Mac couldn't help asking, "Which monstrosity?"

The guy smiled, but didn't take the bait. "Then we razed that old dump of a mall in the spring of 2017."

The other guy said, "Did a damn good job of it, too."

"The construction was all ready to go," said the first guy. "We laid down the infrastructure. We put in some containment girders. We started grading. And then they told us to stop." He made a drunken sound of screeching brakes.

"I blame Mayor McSmiley Face," the second guy said. "He never should have trusted that developer from New York. You can never trust those guys. The mayor was way out of his depth."

"Well, I blame S. D. Ireland," the first guy said. "We trusted the mayor. How stupid was that?"

The second guy said, "You've got a point there. They knew our paychecks would depend on this thing. Plus, look at that hole in the ground! Anybody coming to Burlington this year, what do they get? No farmers market, no downtown mall, and a big freakin' lot full of moon rocks right in the middle of town!" He turned to Mac. "Who do *you* blame?"

"Everybody who's in power," Mac said. "From the Monstrosity-in-Chief right down to the mayor's chihua-hua. Selfish dickwads, every one."

"Now you're talking," the first guy said. They got another beer.

Mac got home late that night. He was prepared to find the doors locked and to climb up the trellis to the sec-ond-floor porch on the back of the house, where he could flake out on the old day-bed. It was actually better for sleeping on these hot summer nights than the study where he had been camped out on a fold-out couch ever since he had moved back in. But no, the kitchen door was unlocked, and there at the table, under the hanging lamp, sat Rowan, eating a bowl of cereal. He was still wearing the green hoodie.

Mac stood by the table. "Cap'n Crunch?" he said.

"Don't tell your wife," Rowan said. "Your daughter got 'em for me at Cumby's."

Mac raised his eyebrows.

"Next time," said Rowan, "I gotta ask her to get me some real milk." He grimaced at the brick-like carton of soy milk.

"I feel you," said Mac. "Where is everybody?"

"Well, your wife, she goes to bed early. But you knew that. Your daughter came in for a while with that River dude, and then they went out again."

"And the other guys?"

Rowan's voice was clear as a clarinet. "They went back to town."

Mac looked at their reflections in the back window of the kitchen.

Rowan added, "I'm staying here."

"I see," said Mac. He could feel his hamstrings tighten.

"You know that little room off the front porch?"

"The sun room?"

"I guess. We put a cot in there."

"OK," said Mac. What could he say? It wasn't his house anymore.

"But I can't sleep this early, you know?"

"Well," Mac said, "I can. Turn out the light when you're done. Ruth hates it when we leave lights burning for no reason." He went down the hall to his fold-out couch. But he didn't sleep much.

The next day, things started appearing in the back yard. A truck dropped a stack of mattresses, piled up on the grass by the old wading pool. Some of them were stained and sagging; some of them looked nearly new. Mac was sure they were smothering some toadstools, but such was the havoc and calamity of nature.

The day after that, there was a truckload of old lawn chairs, checkered nylon fraying on its metal tubing. Leaning against the garage was an array of colorful umbrellas—beach umbrellas, golf umbrellas, furled but ready to serve and protect. Next to them was another stack of mattresses. At the kitchen table, Ruth and the Randos schemed. Mac walked into town.

When he got there, he found that City Hall Park had finally been shut down. It was surrounded by a six-foot-high cyclone fence, with signs saying "Sidewalk Closed" and arrows directing you anywhere but here. Mac looped his fingers into the wire diamonds and gazed into the deep shade of trees that were, according to the worst reports, soon to be leveled in favor of more concrete. On Front Porch Forum, people said they just wanted to get the homeless out of the park. But why would they want to do that? Wouldn't those people just go be homeless somewhere else? Like Louise Street?

On the broad pavement in front of the Flynn Theatre, a couple of bodies lay under blankets spread above panels of cardboard. How could they sleep? Traffic rattled by. The day was already hot, fetid with odors from bins in front of Ahli Baba's and the Kountry Kitchen. Nobody knew how to spell. Across the street, a guy in a bright yellow vest used a hand-held drill to drive in the last rivets of the new cyclone fence. It made a brain-shaking roar. The bodies didn't stir. Mac wondered if he knew them.

At the Lamplighter, he saluted the oldest customer and took a seat at the bar. After a while, the S. D. Ireland guys came in and joined him. They were still upset. But Mac could tell that they kind of enjoyed their indignation. He got them a second beer.

The next day, the first of the above-ground swimming pools landed in the back yard. When Mac looked out the kitchen window, it was just there, like an alien spacecraft, lurking beyond a stack of mattresses. What the h-e-double hockey sticks? The next time Mac looked out there, after pouring a cup of coffee and wiping his eyes, a couple of the Randos were dismantling the pool, stacking its heavy plastic components against the shed, folding the flexible nylon floor as neat as a bedsheet. Then one of the guys started swearing and swatting all around his head with flailing palms, and took off running out of the yard. Mac laughed into his coffee mug. Bees.

When another pool arrived, already dismantled this time, and then another, he finally stepped out to chat with one of the Randos who was out there stacking things up. By now, there were six or eight piles of mattresses, dozens of lawn chairs, and a slew of bright umbrellas.

"What's with all the stuff?" Mac asked.

"It's all part of the plan," the guy said. He was a stringy little man with a snub nose and antic brown eyes.

"The plan?"

"Yeah," the man said with guttural relish. "Isn't it great?"

"Um, yeah. What is it?"

The man scrutinized Mac with a squint. "Oh," he said, "if you don't know, I can't tell you."

"But if I knew, then you wouldn't *have* to tell me."

"Now you're getting all logical."

"I like logic."

"Well, good luck with that," the man said, and turned back to stacking up panels. The yard looked like a construction site for a life-size Lego empire.

"What the hell," Mac muttered. He zigged between two piles of mattresses to the old shed, in a far corner of the yard. Inside, there was just enough space for a lawn chair, where, when he closed the door, he could sit quietly in the dusk, looking at the frame of sunlight etched by the ill-fitting door. He didn't need any light to find the bottle of Maker's Mark on a high shelf, next to a rusting trowel. He cleaned the shot glass on an untucked end of his t-shirt.

By and by, he found Ruth holding counsel in the kitchen, with Rowan and three of the Randos at the table. Harper and River were sitting on stools at the breakfast bar, both of them thumbing their phones. Mac sat on the remaining stool, next to River, who looked up and said, "Hi, Mr. McKenzie." River, who used they/them pronouns now, shook their dark shoulder-length hair.

"What's up?" said Mac.

"We've got a gig tomorrow night at Nectar's," said River. "We're just getting the word out."

River played guitar in a band called The Darling

Buds, which seemed to be getting some traction in town.

Mac nodded. Then he spoke to the room. "So," he said, "what's the plan?"

Rowan, still in the green hoodie, looked up from the table. "City Place," he said. "We've got a new design." He pointed to a large sheet of white butcher's paper on the table, and Mac stood to get a better look. It was a neatly drawn map of the empty lot where the mall used to be. Mac pointed to a quadrant full of penciled rectangles in rows. "What are these?" he asked.

"That's the dormitory," said Snubnose.

"Oh," Mac said. "And these big circles?" There were five of them scattered around the lot.

"Swimming pools," said Merle. Shirtless, his tattoos made him look like a superhero on a coffee break.

"Of course," Mac said. "And the smaller circles?"

"Umbrellas!" said Snubnose. You'd fry in there with no shade."

"Right," said Mac. "I guess you haven't drawn in all the lawn chairs."

"They're under the umbrellas," said Merle.

"How are you going to fill the pools with water?"

There was a brief silence. "We're working on that," said Snubnose. Ruth still hadn't spoken.

Mac pointed to a large empty oval in the middle of the lot. "What goes here?"

"Ah," said Snubnose, "That's the centerpiece."

"The pièce de la résistance," said Merle. His accent was good. Maybe he was a Quebecker.

"Roller rink in summer," said Rowan with the clarinet voice, "ice rink in winter. Big Christmas tree in the middle."

"And one of those Jewish candle thingies," said Snubnose.

"Cool," said Mac. "But—" He trailed off.

"But what?" said Snubnose. He was spoiling for a fight.

"But the terrain in there is rocky and uneven," said Mac. "How could anyone skate on it?"

Nobody said anything.

"For that matter," Mac said, "How are you going to get all that stuff in there? I mean, it's surrounded by fences. I'm sure the cops watch it. Even if you had a whole flotilla of trucks to deliver stuff, there's no way they'd let you set it up."

"First you have to dream it," said Merle.

Mac looked at Ruth. She looked tired, but her eyes were bright with purpose. "One thing at a time," she said. "Everything will come together."

The Randos nodded urgently. Harper and River thumbed. A chickadee harked in the yard. Mac went down the hall to the study.

That evening, he stayed in. He looked at one of his old books about polar expeditions and wondered why he had ever been drawn to them. Those guys were nutbirds. They risked their lives for the thrill and glory of being the first to arrive at an imaginary point on the tundra, a place no one wanted to be, where they'd die if they stayed too long. Some of them did die. Their bones crystallized in the ice.

One thing he had come to like about sleeping in this ground-floor room: listening to the noises of the house. He sat in the big armchair with Ruth's laptop in his lap, but mostly he just listened. He heard Harper come and go, off to a dinner shift at Pho Hong, her sneakers brisk and rubbery on the stairs. He heard Ruth go up to bed, early. She ran her nightly bath, and when she moved in it, the tub made squelching sounds. Later, he heard someone come into the kitchen and go to the refrigerator — it must be Rowan. A hallway fan clicked on and started to hum. Then someone went into the hall bathroom, right next to the study where Mac sat, and turned on the shower. It whined in the night. The clarinet voice cried, "Hot, hot, hot." Or was it "Hurt, hurt, hurt"? And then it seemed to be sobbing. Over the rush of the water, it was hard to tell. Then the water shut off with a clunk, and the human voice continued. Sobbing, then silence.

Eventually, Mac heard someone leaving the bathroom and going on down the hall to the kitchen. He got up from his armchair and followed, barefoot.

At the kitchen table, under the hanging lamp, there was Rowan, wearing a t-shirt and jeans. Without the hoodie, it was painfully clear how thin he was — praying mantis thin. When Mac stepped in, Rowan was focused on the map. Across the top of his shaved head, from one ear to a keloid lump at the crown, there was a gleaming pink scar.

Mac cleared his throat, and Rowan looked up.

"You OK, man?"

Rowan looked at him for a long moment. Then he said, "Yeah. I got some aches." He paused. "You?"

Mac said, "I'm OK." He looked at his hands and flexed the fingers. "Maybe a little arthritis."

What a stupid thing to say. But Rowan brightened, and laughed. "I hear you, man."

Mac kept flexing his fingers. Rock, paper, rock, paper.

"Rest," said Rowan. "That's the thing. Nobody sleeps enough."

Mac said, "Right. Thanks. Good night." And went back down the hall.

The plan was crazy, of course. But so is the sky, so full of stars you can't see in the daytime. So is the underside of a big flat rock at the creek when you're a boy, the mud teeming with mites and bugs that curl up so you can't get at them. So is a park in the middle of town, a park rich with shade trees on a hot July afternoon, trees you can't sit under because a big ugly fence says Oh no you don't. It was crazy that the government was threatening to carry out raids on peaceful residents in cities all over the country. It was all crazy. Mac walked up to the Lamplighter the next afternoon and took a seat by their oldest customer. He ordered seltzer. The cool fizz tickled his nose. After a while, the S. D. Ireland boys came in.

Late that afternoon, when Mac got home, Evie Morrison was out in the garden again. Mac lingered at the curb. Leah was arranging a sprinkler. The weather had been dry for weeks.

"Those guys creep me out," Evie said. "I'm sorry, I can't help it."

"Why?" Mac asked. "What are they doing?"

"Nothing. That's just it. They sit in the front yard, or on the jungle gym down in the park, smoking and talking and playing that god-awful metal music. Doing nothing. Elly Taylor says some of them have been arrested for burglary."

"Oh," said Mac, "so Elly has seen their rap sheets?"

"It was on Front Porch Forum," said Evie.

"Ah, then it must be true," Mac said.

Evie gave him the eye. Leah came up with a hose in her hand, looking like an ornamental heron. "They have to go somewhere," she said. "Now that City Hall Park is shut down."

Mac said, "That's right. The parks are public property."

"I know," Evie sighed. "I'm a bad person. It just makes me anxious, OK?" She picked up her bucket of weeds, and Leah turned on the sprinkler. In the late-afternoon sun, it hung the world with mist.

That evening, Mac walked into town again. It had been a drag to sell his old truck, but man, he was getting his exercise. What would he do when winter brought its ten-below-zero days? That was too far away to fret about now. Now it was a fine July evening, eighty degrees and a breeze. He made his way to Nectar's.

He couldn't claim to understand the music made by the Darling Buds. Sometimes it was plain old rock and roll, three-chord greetings from Asbury Park. But just when he had settled into that groove, the drummer and the bass dropped into a background shoosh, and River drubbed out a monotone on guitar, whispering unintelligibly into the mike, then made a Yoko Ono yelp, and then, of a sudden, slinked into a Robert Johnson blues. "You better come on in my kitchen," River cajoled. "There's going to be rain outdoors."

Maybe Mac wasn't supposed to get it. Maybe it wasn't for him, and that was OK. Somebody was getting it: the room was mostly full. He couldn't say that he was entirely at ease with the fact that River was wearing a skirt and eye shadow, and he, Mac, got all tangled up trying to refer to River as "them" — but why did Mac have to be the measure of all things? River was Harper's friend, that's all he needed to know. There she was across the room, standing close to the little low stage, long blond hair trailing down a black t-shirt to the waist of her short jean shorts.

Mac knew that if he went over there, he would be greeted coolly. This broke his heart.

But what were hearts for? Hearts were for breaking and mending and breaking again. Life was more like a country song than he would ever have believed.

Still, Nectar's made him happy. He liked the gravy fries. He liked the crowd, motley and sloppy, a little unpredictable. They could turn on a band that was mailing it in. He liked the big garage-style window, open to the Main Street sidewalk on a warm summer night. He didn't even look up at the TV screen over the bar to see how the Red Sox were doing. Tonight, he had a mission.

Over by the window, far from the stage, alone at a little round table, sat Ted Balakian. A heavy-set man in khakis and a blue button-down, he had a square jaw and well-tended black hair scraped back from a high forehead. Mac had seen him at this table before, on a night when the Buds were playing. He was hunched over a tall glass of something clear, with a wedge of lime. He gazed at the band while they hammer-and-tonged a song about fritters, or critters, or craters. Enunciation was not their forte.

Ted was River's father. They lived in an apartment complex on Pine Street, just down the hill from Ruth's neighborhood. River's mother had left them long ago, back when River was still known as Josh, king of the skate park. Now River and Harper were—what, exactly? Mac didn't know. Harper wasn't confiding in him these days. Keeping up with her was like flying over cities at night, beautiful and baffling. River worked a day job with Ted, a foreman at the S. D. Ireland Co.

While the Buds wailed about wisdom teeth, or maybe it was grizzled feet, Mac made his way to the little round table, made eye contact with Ted, and gestured at an empty chair beside it. Ted nodded and spread an open palm at the chair. Mac set his beer on the table and sat, and the two men watched the band.

After a while, the Buds took a break. In the sudden silence, talk blossomed all over the room. But not between these men. They sat like bookends without any books between them. Cars glimmered by on Main Street, windows open, radios dopplering past. Finally, Mac spoke.

"Listen, Ted. I have a proposition for you."

Two weeks later, it was early August, and everyone was at the empty lot. Only it wasn't empty now. Someone had unpadlocked and swung open the gates where big machinery could roll in. Someone had set up several portable swimming pools, and filled them with water. Over in the southwest corner, someone had laid out a host of mattresses. Lawn chairs popped up everywhere, shaded by rumbustious beach umbrellas. In the center of it all, someone had laid down an oval of new concrete. A row of portable toilets stood at attention by the Cherry Street curb. Across the cloudless summer sky, a crane dangled its empty hook.

It wasn't Utopia. There were syringes among the mattresses. There was a fist-fight over someone peeing in a pool. Some of these people still had no homes, and this was no solution. But there were also kids splashing. There were Rowan and Merle and Snubnose, teetering around on old roller blades donated by the Y. There were Evie and Leah, planting late-summer flowers in a raised bed at the center of the oval — zinnias, cosmos, snapdragons, given by Gardener's Supply. And there were Harper and River with their old pals Breiner and Ronan, up on ladders leaned against the sawed-off end of the old mall, unfurling a hand-lettered banner that welcomed everyone to People's Park.

At first, the mayor declared that the whole action was illegal. They had no permits, he said. It was private property, owned by the developer. But he didn't say what the city was going to do about it. He said it was under review. What could they do? Send in the cops? Hauling kids out of pools wouldn't look good in the media. Besides, S. D. Ireland had dozens of city contracts; the mayor wouldn't want to mess with them. Some people said he was actually delighted about the whole operation. Instead of being the mayor who had foolishly trusted the big developer, he was presiding over Burlington being its irrepressible populist self. And while the kids splashed, no one was paying attention to the trees going down in City Hall Park.

But what would happen, a reporter asked Ruth, when the developer asserted his rights, as he would surely do, and shut the whole thing down?

Ruth was sitting in the shade of a Cinzano umbrella, her back to a wall of shredded masonry. Her skin was almost translucent. Mac sat nearby at a splintery picnic table, nursing the world's last beer.

"Then," he heard her say, "We'll begin again."

The Bear's Bris

In the bad old days of treatments, when the nurses were always hanging plastic sacks of toxic stuff above her, Ruth called herself the bag lady. She called herself a chemo sapien; she called herself Chemo Sabe. Mac didn't know if he should laugh or cry.

She was beyond chemo now, so she could eat again. If only she could swallow. Her throat was misbehaving. Mac and Harper, their nineteen-year-old daughter, puréed everything. The whir of the blender was the bass line of these days. Kale, bananas, yogurt, wheat germ, kelp: you could put anything in a smoothie. If only she had an appetite. How do you work up an appetite lying in bed all day? You work up bed sores. Mac and Harper had been instructed to make sure she change position regularly. She called this "sickbed Kama sutra." When they moved her, they asked her if it hurt. Only when I breathe, she said. She swore that if she ever found a comfortable position, she'd never move again.

Looking down at the white sheet draping her torso, she said she missed the landscape of her chest. I've been strip-mined, she said. I've been clear-cut. I'm one stream-lined mama-rama. You could grease me up and shoot me from a cannon. But don't. Gunpowder makes me sneeze.

Laugh, she said. For God's sake.

And then she stopped talking. The throat thing. Radiation moves in mysterious ways. She blinked once for Yes. For No, she scowled like Mrs. Grundy, her kindergarten teacher. Some things never die.

But there was still a moment every day when her throat let up on her and allowed her to speak. It was the first hour after waking, which came before dawn. You could set a clock by her: at five a.m., she was ready to chat. She called this hour Question Time, as if she was Prime Minister. Most days, this hour came near the end of Mac's overnight shift. Harper was still in her bed down the hall, after waiting tables until midnight at Pho Hong. Rowan, the homeless guy who was living in their house these days, was fine with the afternoon.

Growing up as an only child in suburban New Jersey, Ruth spent hours looking under rocks down at the creek. Mites and bugs and worms: what a world. At college in the eighties, she was a Bio major when the other girls were reading *Jane Eyre*. She read it and thought, "Don't marry the crippled guy!" Ten years later, she married a librarian who was sound of limb and eye. They settled in their college town and had their only child, who danced on her father's shoe tops. Ruth started the Environmental Studies program. Mac told the bedtime stories.

Years passed. Ruth fought for the bike path extension and for protection of wetlands near the lake. She led protests against the corporate greedheads who were intent on filling Burlington with high-end housing and chain stores. She wanted Burlington to be its own wonky western New England self, with foreign films and neighborhood theatres and locally owned shops, a taste of the woods and a tang of Quebec. She masterminded the community garden in the park down the street from their South End home. She lived on e-mail and kombucha.

When the first bout of cancer came, she soldiered through it, driving herself to infusions, keeping up with her teaching and campus work. She tried not to burden her husband and daughter, who was ten at the time. She got through it, and focused afresh, twice-born, on her work. There was so much to do. The planet was in mortal danger. Harper was steaming into the mysteries of middle school, too busy for her busy mother. Mac was skating along as always, following sports, reading long books about polar expeditions, managing his library job with a minimum of fuss. And then one October morning he took off, leaving a note about how this was best for them all, leaving Ruth to cope with Harper, leaving no forwarding address. Leaving was his middle name.

Ruth doubled down. She fought the proposal for a massive multi-use development in a central city block. She fought the renovation of City Hall Park, which would bring down trees and spread more cement. She fought the smiling, development-happy mayor. She fought the university, which wasn't happy to find her always in the local news, aggravating rifts between town and gown. She befriended the homeless people who had hung out in the park before the backhoes began to tear it up. Harper, meanwhile, was raised by wolves, and a boyfriend or two.

After six years of wandering, Mac came back. You couldn't say he came "home," because it wasn't his home anymore. He was like an errant uncle, sleeping on the sofa in the study while he got his shit together. At forty-eight, it was a bit late for shit-gathering. Evie Morrison, the neighbor across the street, told Ruth she was crazy to take him in. But Ruth was well into Cancer 2.0 by then, and she wasn't in the business of turning people away. He was out of money. He was out of work. His daughter barely spoke to him. But he was willing to sell his old gas-guzzling truck; that was enough of a down payment for Ruth.

And then, after the big People's Park protest, in which she and her comrades essentially took back the commons by commandeering a city block that was in limbo while awaiting development, her white blood cells went AWOL. Her throat constricted. Her eyesight dimmed. She said the whole world looked like it was painted by Monet. Thank God it wasn't Pollack. She had something called a paraneoplastic condition: her body was attacking itself. She called it a paraneo-Nazi condition. It was setting up a puppet government in the south of France.

It was gerrymandering Wisconsin and North Carolina. It was running for re-election.

Mac and Harper gave each other a wide berth. Rowan, a tall black guy who always wore a green hoodie, was sleeping in the sun room. A bunch of his friends, apparently homeless, too, hung out in the kitchen and the little front yard. Evie and Leah started bringing casseroles Ruth would never eat. Silverman, her old comrade from the barricades, brought news of the latest projects. Nosy old Elly Taylor from down the block, whom Ruth called her "Front Porch Forum Live," brought news of the neighborhood. What a world. Everyone, everyone, wanted to help. The miracle was that she let them.

There is no rising action in this story. There is only a person dying.

At first, they put her in the sun room, because it was on the ground floor. It being August, Rowan could sleep on the old day-bed on the second-floor back porch.

The trouble with the sun room was that it was the sun room. The house was not air-conditioned. The morning light, so welcome in January, sliced in through the maples and pin oaks that fronted on Louise Street, making the sun room bake. They closed the blinds; it baked in the dark. She sweated and said nothing. One hot afternoon, Mac saw her grimace, and asked, "Would upstairs be better?" She blinked.

That evening he and Rowan carried her back up the narrow stairs to her old bedroom. Her compact body, once so firm and round, had become light as soufflé. Mac feared that if they bumped her against the bannister, pieces of her would bark off. But she made it intact. She didn't need to be on the ground floor. There was a bathroom on the upstairs hall, with the old tub that might bring her extra comfort now. They put a mini-fridge in her room, and a little collection of plates and cutlery. It was like being in college again.

The room suited her. This was where she had slept for twenty years, first with Mac and then, when he absconded, alone. Her dreams crowded the lintels and windowpanes. On a plain desk against the southern wall, there were stacks of printouts and magazines about glaciers and methane and footprints of all kinds. Projects uncompleted, projects unbegun, moments waiting for their moment. On the wall above them, a still-life by Cezanne. How did he see such greens and blues and lavenders in apples and peaches?

Mac set an electric fan in the eastern window and trained it on her bed. She gave him a big Mrs. Grundy. He turned it off. She Grundied some more. He turned it on again and angled it away from her. She smiled and blinked. Along with the breeze and the steady hum, birdsong filtered into the room. The high scree of swifts, the chatter of swallows.

Rowan moved back to the sun room. On a good day, they wheeled her out to the back porch and laid her on the day bed. She gazed at the old apple tree in the back yard, small green fruits coming on. Some of them fell to the grass with little thuds. Ruth had always been the one to pick them up and chuck them in the compost. Now they drew a dance of bees.

There weren't many good days. There weren't many days. Time moshed and slewed; August pulsed on. They put a cot in the corner of her bedroom, so someone could be at hand all night. Usually, it was Mac. There wasn't much he could do — bring her water in a cup with a bending straw, empty the bed pan. Moisten her lips with a cool, damp cloth that they kept in a cobalt-blue ceramic bowl. Talk to her, read to her, turn on the bedside radio, turn it off when the news was bad. The news was almost always bad.

But some moments were exceedingly sweet. During Question Time some mornings, when the air through her windows was hushed with dew, she spoke about the latest projects so vividly that Mac almost forgot she was sick. How could she still care what happened on that godforsaken city block? Afternoons, Rowan reported on the encampment she had helped organize on the stalled construction site, where homeless people were sacked out on donated mattresses and splashing in above-ground swimming pools. It was political performance art, and the chief performer had been Ruth. Now she couldn't be there, but like any good teacher she understood that the best success takes place after the teacher is gone. The developer was reportedly snared in funding shortfalls, and the mayor was nowhere to be seen. Rowan said the sunflowers Evie and Leah had planted in the makeshift central garden of the rocky lot were now towering twelve feet high. Ruth smiled.

Sometimes in the night she moaned, and Mac didn't know what to do. When he asked in the morning, she said, "It's only moaning. You don't have to do anything."

They kept a pad of paper and a pen by her bed. When they asked if they could bring her anything, she wrote, "Social justice." Then she picked up the pad again. "And time."

There is no conflict in this story. There is only a person dying.

She no longer had the energy to keep up with her e-mail, so Mac tried to manage it for her. The messages poured in. Reports from the encampment downtown. Queries from students who noticed that her courses for the fall had been cancelled. Invitations to all the semester-opening meetings and ceremonies. Calls for papers. Phishing scams. Offers of help from colleagues. Communications from the lawyer who was overseeing the transfer of her late mother's New Jersey house to the woman who had been their maid for twenty years. Mac deleted, deleted, deleted. When he saw a solic-itous note from Ruth's old nemesis, Jocelyn Winters, the ranking Sociology professor who had once tried to block the formation of the Environmental Studies program, and had come on to Mac in the process, he was tempted to answer in words of flint. He made the message vanish.

Without his truck, Mac felt unhorsed, nailed to the house on Louise Street. He did some odd jobs for his old friend Stan, who ran a home-care agency in the Old North End, and Stan paid him under the table, five crisp twenties a week. Then he bought a used bicycle from the Old Spokes Home. It had a schoolboy's bell on the handlebars and matching wire baskets in back. After Question Time, when Harper took over Ruth duty, he lit out on errands, or just to take the air.

August kept pelting by. Long morning shadows stretched down the bricks of Church Street, where tables and chairs were stacked and cabled together, legs up, like interstellar insects. When he rode over the ornamental circles depicting the two hemispheres in stone, in front of City Hall, loose tiles wobbled and clicked. Some mornings brought quick showers that pattered on his Red Sox cap. Afternoons sulked in late-summer heat, but as darkness fell, he could feel the spearmint of autumn coming. He picked up groceries every day, a few at a time, like a good Parisian. Peaches from Pennsylvania Dutch country. Strawberries from Mazza's farm in nearby Colchester, purple heart plums and greengages from an orchard in Shelburne. Blueberries from any hillside where they kept the grackles at bay. He washed them at the kitchen sink and laid them out in a boat-shaped wooden bowl that he set on the table by Ruth's bed. The heat of July still pulsed under the skins. Ruth could eat none of it; it ran straight through her. But she smiled at the offering. Her watchers ate fruit all night and day.

She didn't eat much of anything. The doctors and hospice nurses recommended protein. She had not eaten flesh in thirty years. Mac tried all the tricks of his short-order days: eggs scrambled and coddled and poached, hard-boiled and soft, on toast, in a cup, flat on a plate, *un oeuf sur plat*, as if they were at the zinc counter of a gritty Paris café. She smiled and ate nothing. Harper made her smoothies—yogurt, kale from the community garden, bananas, wheat germ, whey powder. Her mother smiled and took a fairy sip. Rowan brought her poutine from Nectar's, filling her room with fragrant clouds of oil and salt. He said, "Cheese curds are protein, right?" She ate several bites greedily, and he grinned a rare grin. Twenty minutes later, she shat it all out. Rowan changed her diaper.

Out on his bike, Mac hated the people who rode on the sidewalks. Sidewalks were for pedestrians! Then he hated the drivers who made no room for cyclists, and he hated the city for not providing better bicycle routes. He hated the people in all those single-occupant vehicles going their oblivious ways. He hated drivers who turned left at the start of a green light. At the co-op, he hated the people who helped themselves to handfuls of food from the bulk bins. Did they not know that the cost would just be distributed among all the customers, including the ones who didn't steal? And did they not care how unsanitary it was? He hated Starbucks, and all the chains on Church Street. Hated people who started every sentence with the word "So." Hated people, left or right, who thought they had a monopoly on The Truth. There was only one truth, and it was happening in a second-floor bedroom on Louise Street.

One afternoon, he came in from doing errands and went up to that room. It was still Harper's shift, before she headed out to Pho Hong. The sheet of Ruth's bed had been pulled down, and Harper was sitting at the far end, silently rubbing her mother's feet. Mac hated being jealous of his daughter. And of his wife.

Ruth had never been a beauty. She was short and pear-shaped, with a round face and dark frizzy hair that resisted all her teenaged efforts to straighten it, gels and hot irons and lying on her pillow after showering to make it grow flatter. It refused. As a teenager, she lay for hot hours on the chaise longue of her parents' patio, hoping the neighbor's son wasn't peering over the cedar fence at her futile effort to darken her milky skin. Those torpid afternoons resulted in epic burns that flaked and peeled for days, dead skin coming off in swaths until she was perfectly pale again. She cried in exasperation, and cloaked herself in long, loose tunics.

But then she went to study abroad in Paris, and an older man, a Frenchman from Dijon, saw the nervous energy flowing from her. It was nothing if not beautiful. Years later, this happened again in Burlington, when her eyes lit up with projects that would make it a better place to live. There is no greater beauty than purpose engaged.

Mac was no devotee of all her causes — why did compost have to be so messy? — but he couldn't resist the thrum of her.

Now, in her final weeks, the skin was sallow, each movement balked and slow. The bed sores cracked and seeped. Her breath was like old cigarettes. Her flashing dark eyes went hazy. But she listened intently to Rowan's reports on City Place, to Harper's accounts of hijinks at the restaurant, Mac's chat about Stan's unruly clients. Some days, she simply cried. Was it pain? She blinked. Mac set the orange-tinted plastic vial of valium beside the cobalt bowl. "Self-serve," he said. She smiled. Most days, she did not touch it.

In the night, he lay on the cot by the window, waiting for her to ring the little bell that meant she needed him. Cars swished by on Louise Street, coming home late. A garage door clanked shut. Cicadas sang. He watched for the window frames to go pale around the edges of the blinds. The light kept refusing to rise, and refusing to rise. The doctor said sleep would help — but Mac had the impression that she rarely slept. She had terrible gas. Her flatulence rattled like old window blinds. The room smelled of boiled cabbage. In the morning, she said, "I ripped a few good ones last night, didn't I?"

One day, at Ruth's request, Rowan checked in during Question Time. Her voice was low but clear.

"We've got to keep the pressure on," she said. "As long as we have people on the ground, sleeping on the

mattresses and splashing in the pools, it's really the people's property. Just as it always was. The developers
know it would look bad if they try to expel these peaceful squatters. But some day they'll get their act together,
and they'll want to push ahead with their precious monstrosity. That's when we let them know that we're ready
to negotiate. We'll move out *if* they commit fifty per cent
of the residences to lower-income housing. They'll say
no way. We'll hunker down. They'll wait for the cold to
freeze us out. We'll collect coats and blankets and ther-
mal sleeping bags. We'll build fires in fifty-gallon drums.
It's not any colder in that empty lot than in the park, or
under the Flynn marquee. They'll see that we're in it for
the long haul."

Rowan said, "Right on."

Mac hated Rowan.

Evie brought casseroles from across the street. In theory,
they were for Ruth—mac 'n' cheese with extra cheddar,
orzo with green beans and reams of mozzarella. Ruth nib-
bled and smiled her thanks. Later, Mac and Harper and
Rowan found these feasts in the refrigerator. Sometimes,
when their time in the house overlapped, all three of
them sat together at the kitchen table. Except when someone offered to pass a dish, they ate in silence.

Silverman, Ruth's old rabble-rousing compadre, came
with the hospice singers. They stood in a semi-circle around
Ruth's bed and sang "Abide with Me." They sang "A Sprig
of Thyme." They sang "You Can Close Your Eyes." Mac

sat on the windowsill and cried. The day was hot and dry. The ice cream truck tootled by on Louise Street, playing its endless doxology, "It's a Small World After All."

There is no climax in this story. Only a person dying.

Splinters of sunlight through ragged clouds. Mac came in from running errands on his bike leaving his boots by the door. In Ruth's house, you always took off your shoes. Canvas shopping bag in hand, he went straight up to see her. The room was warm and dim. Ruth was napping, as she did more and more often. Harper sat in a straight-back chair on the near side of the bed, focused on her phone. Over by the window, Rowan was reading a thick paperback, leaning forward like the figurehead of a ship. He didn't need to be there; it wasn't his shift yet. As soon as Mac entered, he wanted to go out again, but something held him at the foot of the bed.

"What's the word?" he said softly. He was a little breathless from the stairs.

Harper looked up and shrugged. Rowan nodded from his chair.

Mac raised the bag and whispered, "I got some groceries."

No one said anything. He said, "I should put the perishables in the fridge." Harper nodded. Rowan looked back at his book. "I got some blackberry yogurt," Mac added. "The kind she likes, from Quebec"

Harper lowered the phone to her lap. "Hail the conquering hero," she said.

He gazed at her. She was all angles, from the long

beaky nose that was broken at her birth to the splay of her bony legs, now folded under her. Today her long yellow hair was piled high on her head, giving her a lopsided look. She was wearing a black spandex top that bared her wide shoulders. Spread out across the top of her back, from the base of her neck to the tip of each delt, was a tattoo of a pair of wings, deep blue against rosy flesh. Mac hated tattoos. Why would she want to disfigure herself forever with a teenage whim?

He lowered the shopping bag and nodded at her phone. "Anything good?" he said.

"What?"

"On your phone. Are you streaming something?"

"I was texting my boss to tell him I'll be late."

He looked at his watch. "You don't have to be late. I'm here. And Rowan's here, too, for that matter." But when he looked over to the chair by the window, it was empty. When did Rowan slip out?

"Yeah," she said. "You're here."

She set the phone on the bedside table. "Dad," she said, in a voice he hardly knew. "Why did you leave?"

The room was unbearably hot. The yogurt would spoil. His feet, his stockinged feet, would not move.

He set the bag down. "I," he said. Then he stopped, and started again. "I," he said again. Then he fell silent. He looked at his ungainly daughter. But he couldn't hold her gaze. When his eyes strayed, he saw that Ruth's eyes were open, and fixed on him.

"Ruthie," he said.

His feet stayed put, and he lowered his head. He stood there like that for a long minute, until Harper spoke.

"Never mind," she said, in that strange grownup voice. "You're here now."

He went downstairs. After the dimness of Ruth's room, everything was too bright. The kitchen was too yellow. No one was in it. He put away the groceries. Then he pulled on his boots. He didn't lace them up.

In the back yard, at the picnic table, Rowan sat having a smoke. The yard was a mess. Until Ruth went so sharply downhill a month ago, Mac had been tending to it, cutting the grass and weed-whacking. Now he could hardly see the toadstools through the shaggy grass. In the flower bed by the little patio, gout weed was taking over. A litter of small red leaves had already dropped from the burning bush. He shuffled out and took a seat on the picnic bench facing Rowan. Late-afternoon clouds boiled up in the east. The air was thick as amber.

Mac said, "She doesn't have long now."

Rowan nodded.

"The hospice woman will be here soon."

"Right."

Rowan pulled a pack of cigarettes from his hoodie pouch, tapped it against the edge of the table so a few butts protruded, and held it out to Mac.

Mac said, "No, thanks."

Rowan tilted his head to one side and extended the cigarettes more fully. How did he know? Mac smiled a little, then took one. Rowan gave him a light.

He hadn't had a cigarette in twenty years, since that afternoon in Paris when he and Ruth, not yet married, had split up to spend some alone time. Mac wandered through the Jardin des Plantes, stood agog in front of a stegosaurus at the Museum of Natural History, and sat on a bench in the sandy circle of Les Arènes de Lutèce, a park built on the ruins of a Roman arena. He had told himself that was the right place for his final cigarette.

And it was. Until now. He took a drag, and coughed a little. It was astonishingly good.

"Why do you do this?" he asked Rowan. "Sit for hours by the bed of a dying woman you barely know?"

Rowan ashed his cigarette into the long grass. He spoke slowly, after long pauses. "I had a little room on my calendar," he said. He smiled. "She was good to me." Pause. "Plus, I had a brother who died of cancer."

"What kind?"

Rowan shrugged. "The kind that kills you. I wasn't there."

A silence passed. Then Mac asked, "What will you do next?"

"Next," Rowan said. "That's never been my strong suit." But then he rocked forward, hands on knees, and spoke more quickly, into the grass. "We've got the encampment to keep alive, you know? We'll need to take the swimming pools down soon. Some people say we can get portable heaters like the ones by the outdoor tables at Leunig's, and we can put up plastic awnings, and then we'd bring in more tables and chairs, and create little areas where people can do stuff like play board games. We're talking to people at the Y. You know they're moving into a new building."

Mac nodded.

"So they're going to have all kinds of old equipment, mats and sports gear and exercise machines and stuff, that won't look good in that shiny new place. What will they do with it? We're the handiest recycling possible. It's just a few blocks away. Imagine the caravan on moving day."

Mac imagined it. Borrowed trucks and vans and human hands. Still, he wondered. "Do you really think they'll let you do that? Won't the equipment get rusty over time? Who would use it in the dead of winter?"

"Whoa," Rowan said. "One thing at a time." He ground out his cigarette on a patio brick. "Right now, it's time for my shift upstairs." He went inside.

Mac felt woozy with nicotine. It was a crazy vision. But what the hell. It was better than an abandoned rocky lot.

In a few minutes, Harper came out, spruce in a black Pho Hong t-shirt. She got in the Subaru and drove off.

Darkness was coming on, grains of it gathering in corners of the yard. He knew he ought to go in and get some sleep. In eight hours, his own shift would begin. But he wasn't tired. He sat at the picnic table and listened to the evening noises. Cutlery on a dish next door. An air conditioner churring. The murmur of voices from some other patio.

The sky was salted with stars. They didn't care what was happening on Louise Street. They had things to do.

The next morning in Question Time, Ruth told a joke. More or less. It was five a.m., and the room was still dark. A night light glowed green by the door. Mac was sitting by the bed with her laptop on his knees. The screen had been dark for a while.

"What was that joke?" she said. She was already laughing.

"What joke?"

"The one about the bear."

"The bear."

"You know." She sounded a little wonky. Probably needed to pee. He was ready to put her in the chair for the short trip down the hall. But first things first. She sounded determined.

"A bear escapes from the zoo," she said. He could hear her smile. "They call up a priest, a minister, and a rabbi to help." She paused. "I can't remember what the priest and the minister do." She paused again. "Something." She chuckled. "But it's always the rabbi who matters, right?" She was cracking up now. "Remember?"

He shook his head in the dark. There was a dumb smile on his face.

"OK, OK," she said, "I think I've got it. The rabbi goes out in the woods." She cracked up again. "After a while, he comes out, all dirty, his clothes torn to tatters, with scratches all over his face and arms."

She laughed again, a soft reincarnation of her old donkey laugh. Then she had to catch her breath. He was afraid it would hurt her to laugh like that. But she went on. "The rabbi says, 'Maybe I shouldn't have started with the bris.'"

They both laughed for a minute in the dark. Then Mac picked her up, to put her in the chair. She had wet the bed. There were clean sheets in the hall closet.

That afternoon, Mac came home to find Harper and River kissing. He didn't mean to sneak up on them, but his bicycle was quiet, and they had music on. He stepped into the kitchen and there they were, standing by the stove, twined, oblivious. Harper's hand was cupping River's butt.

Mac wanted to hate it. How could they? He slipped back out the door, then eased it shut and got on the bike again. He rode to the park at the end of their block and did figure eights on the basketball court until he noticed porch lights coming on in the neighborhood.

In the final days, she wanted silence. No fucking news. And no music, either. "Might as well get used to it," she whispered one morning. They listened to the leaves fall on the shingles outside the windows.

It would be September, if anyone was checking. Thunderclouds brimmed and spilled. Apples thudded in the wet yard. Upstairs, everyone gathered. Mac and Harper and Rowan and a tall hospice nurse named Tilly. What a world.

Ruth gestured to Mac with her chin. He leaned in close, bringing his ear to her mouth. But he didn't hear anything. Maybe it wasn't words. Maybe it was a kiss, soft and cool and felt on his skin a long time after.

Things I Want You to Do

It started with easy tasks.

Watch as many sunsets as you can from a swinging bench on the waterfront.

Stand outside of Ben & Jerry's, just to take in the aroma of hot fudge. You don't need the sugar and butterfat, just the smell. This is the fragrance of Burlington.

Go up Mount Philo, any time of year, and linger at the rail looking west across the patchwork of the Champlain Valley. Watch for the swoop of a vulture, a beautiful thing. Remember that they're not predators; they never kill live prey. They are, along with catfish, among the great recyclers.

Frequent all the ethnic places in the Old North End. The Moroccan café. The African grocery. That new taco place. They need you more than the tourist pits of Church Street. If they put up television screens, raise a squawk. Tell them you came for stew, not news. Tell them that stew is the real news.

These commands were written in Ruth's confident hand, in bold black Sharpie, on sheets of paper with random printing on the other side. The letters were large: her eyes were failing. Before long, the tasks became more challenging.

Water the community garden every day in spring, summer, and early fall. Don't let a summer shower talk you out of it. God knows we tried to terrace that hillside, to keep the water from running off, but still. It tends to run downhill. And even if the zucchini is getting enough rain on a given day, you never know what else the plot may need. Weeding. Dead-heading. A little simple encouragement.

Don't tell me now, after all these years, that plants don't need encouragement. Don't make your mother cry.

Buy something every week from Crow, and also from Phoenix Books. Even if it's just a post card. We need our book-stores. They need young people like you making them look hip. Never underestimate the power of sheer presence. Eighty per cent of life, you know.

Try to stand up straighter. I know you learned to slouch in middle school, when you were so much taller than the boys. But there's no reason for it now. I spent my whole life trying to be taller. As if 49 years were a whole life. But you know what I mean. They're what I was given.

Given by what? The universe? Must there have been a giver? I'm not likely to settle this question now. But that doesn't mean I'm going to stop asking it. When you stop asking, you're halfway gone. Too many people are halfway gone all their lives.

Anyway, stand up straighter! Tall women are sexy.

I know you don't want to hear about sexiness from your mother. What does she know? But this is my last memo. I get to say what I want.

Try not to give into rage. It's no earthly good. I know.

She left these sheets with Rowan, the homeless man who sat by her bed every afternoon. Why not entrust them to Mac, her husband, who sat the night shift? Or give them directly to Harper, who relieved him in the morning? The sheets don't say. She gave them to Rowan. He stacked them up.

Honor the places in your life. This isn't always easy to do. For years, I scoffed at suburban New Jersey. It was just where I came from, and I couldn't get away from it fast enough. In college, I made the obligatory japes about "the armpit of the nation"; I even pretended to be from other places. For a while, it was Montreal, although I had never been there. It just sounded so exotic. What a poser I was. When I went back to NJ for your Nana's funeral, I realized that like it or not, I was shaped by that house, those rooms, that middle-class neighborhood. And being a poser was part of it. That skill served me every day as a teacher. I posed as someone who knew what she was talking about — and people seemed to believe it. We are the amalgam of our poses. I'm posing as the wise mother now.

Of course, I honor Paris, too. But probably not in the ways you'd expect — not for beauty or art or haute cuisine. In fact, I ate miserably during that year of study abroad. So many crepes, so much coffee and chocolate and dull little vanilla cookies. I was unhappy so often, I just wanted sugar and caffeine straight to my bloodstream. So my belle époque *wasn't Cordon Bleu and the Louvre. It was the stones of the place, the quais, the music from café doorways. It was the unexpected parks, like Buttes-Chaumont, with its bridges over watery ravines; it was the kiosks on the corners, with so many papers and magazines that you wondered who could have so much to say about the world. It was the sense that someone made this place; it didn't just happen. And if sometimes it was made badly — the highways by the Seine, destroying riverside strolls; the removal of the great market at Les Halles, tearing out the belly of the city; the lifeless towers of the Front de Seine and the Place d'Italie — it could still be remade. They had been doing it forever. And this could be true of other places, too — like Burlington, Vermont. To keep remaking this place became my* raison d'être.

I wish you had lived with us on Murray Street, before you were born. Oh, that apartment wasn't grand; it wasn't even very clean. There were so many years of grime in that kitchen, I could never scrub it enough. The linoleum was, let us charitably say, uninspired. The wallpaper was peeling. Sometimes I pulled off a loose swath, hoping maybe your father would get the message that it needed replacing. But he was so intent on getting out of there, finding a house of our own, that any improvements seemed like a waste of time, effort, and money. You were on the way, and that little apartment wasn't big enough for three of us. Even on bright days — none too numerous in our fair city — that place was dim. Most of the windows faced north, and in the winter they were so drafty that the landlord covered them in plastic, billowy and opaque, which I tore down right away. Better a draft than that underwater feeling. I'll never forget the ticking of those baseboard heaters, and the dry, hot smell. My skin was chapped all that winter. The neighborhood was what passes for urban in Vermont: worn-out wood-frame triple-deckers, dilapidated porches tottering directly over the filthy littered sidewalks, no green space for blocks, and drug deals on the corners, in front of the tired Kwik-Stop and its specials on Big Gulp drinks.

And yet — can you tell from the way I'm rhapsodizing? — I loved that place. Here's why.

One winter morning, I was sitting at the kitchen table, trying to get prepared for a class I would be leading on God knows what — in those early days of my career, it was always seat of the pants, last minute desperation. What could I possibly say about Environmental Studies to students who signed up because it fulfilled a distributional requirement and maybe sounded cool? I thought I had to tell them everything about the history of the discipline, from John Muir to Rachel Carson to Bill McKibben, from the founding of the National Parks to the depredations of fracking. I wanted to make sure they understood that this was real, it was urgent, it was necessary. And of course that was right, but it was also a recipe for high anxiety every time I sat down to that wobbly kitchen table covered with papers and an eggy plate or two — back when I still made eggs for your father and me every morning.

On this particular morning, he must have been out walking Sloppy Joe. It was a bright morning; I remember because of what happened next. Something out the window caught my attention: a toddler, dressed only in a diaper, out in the middle of Murray Street. Barefoot, bare torso, bare arms and head, out on that roughly paved street — "Pothole Paradise," your father called it — and no adult in sight. The child — I couldn't tell if it was a girl or a boy — was standing there, teetering a little, as toddlers do. I was so mesmerized by the strangeness of that vision that I sat and stared. If I thought at all, maybe I thought, "Well, it's just Murray Street; thank goodness it doesn't get much traffic."

But the child was nearly naked, and alone, and all it needed was one car, one driver not quite awake yet, to make a misery beyond fathoming. Before I could move, I heard footsteps clattering down the wooden stairs of our building, and in a moment I saw Ludmila, our upstairs neighbor, a lovely gawky Bosnian refugee, rushing out into the street toward the child. And in that same moment, from two other nearby apartments, two other women were converging on the spot. One had motioned for an approaching car to stop. One had already reached the child, and taken it up in her arms. As Ludmila arrived, they started talking animatedly, and it was easy to imagine: "Do you know whose child this is?" Ludmila had brought a blanket that the other woman wrapped around the baby. Later, still breathless, Ludmila told me how the three women then went door to door, looking for the baby's people. Before long, they found that it belonged to a big Tibetan family down the street, where two other children were sick and the mother was at wit's end tending to them, thinking this one was still in its crib.

It could have happened anywhere. Our sweet neighbors on Louise Street would surely have been as concerned and engaged. But would they have noticed as quickly? They might have been so well ensconced in their cozy back rooms, many of them added in recent renovations, sitting by their woodstoves with NPR, that they wouldn't have been looking until the misery had already taken place. On Murray Street, we were all there, in our mingy kitchen windows, looking out on our little world. Maybe we weren't better people. There was too much alcohol, and opioids, and broken glass on the sidewalks. But we knew if there was a baby in danger.

I went back to my class prep, to Aldo Leopold or whatever I thought my students needed to hear that day. If I had thought about it more fully, I might have realized that the welfare of that baby depended on the density of housing and the design of outward-facing apartments, as well as the availability of women to notice it. Before long, I had decided that this was a vision of environmental studies I wanted to pursue.

Every place on earth is worth honoring, if you care enough.

Start a Little Free Library. Support the Good News Garage. Stay the hell out of Starbucks. I don't care how good the coffee is. What do we mean by "good"?

Pessimism is unethical. Yes, things are bad, and they'll get worse. So? Get to work. Moping never saved a species. Or even a tree. You know what the poet W. S. Merwin says: "If this was the last day of the world, still I would plant a tree."

The Scottish mountaineer W. H. Murray says, "Find beauty. Be still."

I know, I've never been famous for being still. Until now. But before you can do anything, you have to find a stillness in your heart. That's beauty.

OK, I'm getting a little cosmo-rama. But one more quotation. Jonas Salk posed the essential question: "Are we being good ancestors?"

That was the longest entry. It must have taken days. It astonished Rowan that a woman who on some days was barely able to signal yes or no could, when she got going, produce so many pages. Still he kept stacking up the sheets. Mac and Harper had no idea. Ruth kept writing, as long as she was able.

Work with people. And creatures. And things.

People like to say that we live in the Anthropocene now. OK, yes, this is the era in which human activity has marked the planet more than anything else, and the result has been disastrous. So? We have to make it the Symbiocene. You and your generation have to take the forest as our model. Scientists like Suzanne Simard have shown that trees cooperate and communicate through their root systems, that older trees give up nutrients for the sake of younger, weaker trees. Any healthy forest, she says, is a wood-wide web. We need to think of our communities this way. "America First" is a recipe for starvation. We need to work with people everywhere.

This includes your father. After he left — after the shock and some months of baffled dismay — I got a lawyer to rework the deed for our house so as to write him out of it. She just had to show that he had forfeited his claim by clearing out and abandoning us. It wasn't hard to do. Now I'm leaving the house to both of you. I don't know how you'll settle this. But I figure you'll have to talk.

What can I tell you about your father? He's selfish and short-sighted to the point of being cruel, although cruelty is never the intention. I think. He drinks too much. He's insane about baseball. His feet smell like wilty expired spinach, and his socks are worse. Don't volunteer to do his laundry. For all his worldly knowledge — and he's a damn smart man — he's still a farm boy from Addison County, desperate to stay off the farm. He is a romantic in all the worst ways, capable of idolizing those maniacs like Ernest Shackleton who committed icy suicide on polar expeditions, capable of idolizing you to the point that he doesn't really see you. You become a plaster saint, until one day you choose to step down from your pedestal, and he's as disappointed as an eight-year-old whose favorite player just got traded to another team.

How could he walk out on us? Oh, I understand how he could walk out on me. I was so devoted to my work that I was hardly there sometimes; he was longing for more than I wanted to give, and he didn't know how to ask. But walk out on you? At age thirteen? When he had always been the favorite parent? Just when you probably needed him most? Walk out without a goodbye or a forwarding address? How could he do that?

Ask him. He owes you an explanation. It may be wrong to say that you owe him anything, but it would be a kindness to ask. When he fumbles in his effort to respond — as he surely will — give him a day or two, and ask again. There may be no satisfactory answer — it was instinct, it was a male got-to-wander thing, it was what Shackleton would have done — but asking is a way to show you care. He lives in your house. You live in his house.

He is also a romantic in the best ways. He didn't have to

come back. He doesn't have to stay. He loves you beyond all reason. Give him a chance to show it.

I'm putting too much of this in the imperative. Who am I to tell you what to do? I'm a dead woman. I am the past. But you know – I know you know – that we are made of the past. How could it be otherwise? These are the things I want you to do. You don't have to do them.

But do them.

I am giving these sheets to Rowan, to be passed along to you after I'm gone. What are you supposed to do about Rowan? Talk to him. Talk to your father. I have not written Rowan into the will. But you can. The world-wide web begins at home.

There's one more thing I want you to do, dear Harper. Go to one of your places – that little triangle of beach at Lakeside; or the meadow up on Ledge Street, where you can stand looking over the lake; or just the roof outside your bedroom window, where you were forbidden to climb as a child but you did it anyway. Go to one of those places, and be still. And remember that the world, this tiny, fragile world of knuckles and curtains, this speck in the cosmos, our poor blighted home – can be so very wide.

Fomite

About Fomite

A fomite is a medium capable of transmitting infectious organisms from one individual to another.

"The activity of art is based on the capacity of people to be infected by the feelings of others." Tolstoy, *What Is Art?*

Writing a review on Amazon, Good Reads, Shelfari, Library Thing or other social media sites for readers will help the progress of independent publishing. To submit a review, go to the book page on any of the sites and follow the links for reviews. Books from independent presses rely on reader-to-reader communications.

For more information or to order any of our books, visit:
http://www.fomitepress.com/

More Titles from Fomite...

Novels
Joshua Amses — *During This, Our Nadir*
Joshua Amses — *Ghatsr*
Joshua Amses — *Raven or Crow*
Joshua Amses — *The Moment Before an Injury*
Jaysinh Birjepatel — *Nothing Beside Remains*
Jaysinh Birjepatel — *The Good Muslim of Jackson Heights*
David Brizer — *Victor Rand*
Paula Closson Buck — *Summer on the Cold War Planet*
Dan Chodorkoff — *Loisaida*
David Adams Cleveland — *Time's Betrayal*
Jaimee Wriston Colbert — *Vanishing Acts*
Roger Coleman — *Skywreck Afternoons*
Marc Estrin — *Hyde*
Marc Estrin — *Kafka's Roach*
Marc Estrin — *Speckled Vanities*
Zdravka Evtimova — *In the Town of Joy and Peace*
Zdravka Evtimova — *Sinfonia Bulgarica*
Daniel Forbes — *Derail This Train Wreck*
Peter Fortunato — *Carnevale*
Greg Guma — *Dons of Time*
Richard Hawley — *The Three Lives of Jonathan Force*
Lamar Herrin — *Father Figure*
Michael Horner — *Damage Control*
Ron Jacobs — *All the Sinners Saints*
Ron Jacobs — *Short Order Frame Up*
Ron Jacobs — *The Co-conspirator's Tale*
Scott Archer Jones — *And Throw Away the Skins*

Fomite

Scott Archer Jones — *A Rising Tide of People Swept Away*
Julie Justicz — *Degrees of Difficulty*
Maggie Kast — *A Free Unsullied Land*
Darrell Kastin — *Shadowboxing with Bukowski*
Coleen Kearon — *#triggerwarning*
Coleen Kearon — *Feminist on Fire*
Jan English Leary — *Thicker Than Blood*
Diane Lefer — *Confessions of a Carnivore*
Rob Lenihan — *Born Speaking Lies*
Douglas W. Milliken — *Our Shadows' Voice*
Colin Mitchell — *Roadman*
Ilan Mochari — *Zinsky the Obscure*
Peter Nash — *Parsimony*
Peter Nash — *The Perfection of Things*
George Ovitt — *Stillpoint*
George Ovitt — *Tribunal*
Gregory Papadoyiannis — *The Baby Jazz*
Pelham — *The Walking Poor*
Andy Potok — *My Father's Keeper*
Frederick Ramey — *Comes a Time*
Joseph Rathgeber — *Mixedbloods*
Kathryn Roberts — *Companion Plants*
Robert Rosenberg — *Isles of the Blind*
Fred Russell — *Rafi's World*
Ron Savage — *Voyeur in Tangier*
David Schein — *The Adoption*
Lynn Sloan — *Principles of Navigation*
L.E. Smith — *The Consequence of Gesture*
L.E. Smith — *Travers' Inferno*
L.E. Smith — *Untimely RIPped*
Bob Sommer — *A Great Fullness*
Tom Walker — *A Day in the Life*
Susan V. Weiss —*My God, What Have We Done?*
Peter M. Wheelwright — *As It Is On Earth*
Suzie Wizowaty — *The Return of Jason Green*

Poetry
Anna Blackmer — *Hexagrams*
Antonello Borra — *Alfabestiario*
Antonello Borra — *AlphaBetaBestiaro*
Antonello Borra — *Fabbrica delle idee/The Factory of Ideas*
L. Brown — *Loopholes*
Sue D. Burton — *Little Steel*
Christine Butterworth-McDermott — *Evelyn As*
David Cavanagh— *Cycling in Plato's Cave*
James Connolly — *Picking Up the Bodies*

Fomite

Greg Delanty — *Loosestrife*
Mason Drukman — *Drawing on Life*
J. C. Ellefson — *Foreign Tales of Exemplum and Woe*
Tina Escaja/Mark Eisner — *Caida Libre/Free Fall*
Anna Faktorovich — *Improvisational Arguments*
Barry Goldensohn — *Snake in the Spine, Wolf in the Heart*
Barry Goldensohn — *The Hundred Yard Dash Man*
Barry Goldensohn — *The Listener Aspires to the Condition of Music*
R. L. Green — *When You Remember Deir Yassin*
Gail Holst-Warhaft — *Lucky Country*
Raymond Luczak — *A Babble of Objects*
Kate Magill — *Roadworthy Creature, Roadworthy Craft*
Tony Magistrale — *Entanglements*
Gary Mesick — *General Discharge*
Andreas Nolte — *Mascha: The Poems of Mascha Kaléko*
Sherry Olson — *Four-Way Stop*
Brett Ortler — *Lessons of the Dead*
Aristea Papalexandrou/Philip Ramp — *Μας προσπερνά/It's Overtaking Us*
Janice Miller Potter — *Meanwell*
Janice Miller Potter — *Thoreau's Umbrella*
Philip Ramp — *The Melancholy of a Life as the Joy of Living It Slowly Chills*
Joseph D. Reich — *A Case Study of Werewolves*
Joseph D. Reich — *Connecting the Dots to Shangrila*
Joseph D. Reich — *The Derivation of Cowboys and Indians*
Joseph D. Reich — *The Hole That Runs Through Utopia*
Joseph D. Reich — *The Housing Market*
Kenneth Rosen and Richard Wilson — *Gomorrah*
Fred Rosenblum — *Vietnumb*
David Schein — *My Murder and Other Local News*
Harold Schweizer — *Miriam's Book*
Scott T. Starbuck — *Carbonfish Blues*
Scott T. Starbuck — *Hawk on Wire*
Scott T. Starbuck — *Industrial Oz*
Seth Steinzor — *Among the Lost*
Seth Steinzor — *To Join the Lost*
Susan Thomas — *In the Sadness Museum*
Susan Thomas — *The Empty Notebook Interrogates Itself*
Paolo Valesio/Todd Portnowitz — *La Mezzanotte di Spoleto/Midnight in Spoleto*
Sharon Webster — *Everyone Lives Here*
Tony Whedon — *The Tres Riches Heures*
Tony Whedon — *The Falkland Quartet*
Claire Zoghb — *Dispatches from Everest*

Stories
Jay Boyer — *Flight*
L. M Brown — *Treading the Uneven Road*

Fomite

Michael Cocchiarale — *Here Is Ware*
Michael Cocchiarale — *Still Time*
Neil Connelly — *In the Wake of Our Vows*
Catherine Zobal Dent — *Unfinished Stories of Girls*
Zdravka Evtimova —*Carts and Other Stories*
John Michael Flynn — *Off to the Next Wherever*
Derek Furr — *Semitones*
Derek Furr — *Suite for Three Voices*
Elizabeth Genovise — *Where There Are Two or More*
Andrei Guriuanu — *Body of Work*
Zeke Jarvis — *In A Family Way*
Arya Jenkins — *Blue Songs in an Open Key*
Jan English Leary — *Skating on the Vertical*
Larry Lefkowitz — *Enigmatic Tales*
Marjorie Maddox — *What She Was Saying*
William Marquess — *Boom-shacka-lacka*
Gary Miller — *Museum of the Americas*
Jennifer Anne Moses — *Visiting Hours*
Martin Ott — *Interrogations*
Christopher Peterson — *Amoebic Simulacra*
Jack Pulaski — *Love's Labours*
Charles Rafferty — *Saturday Night at Magellan's*
Ron Savage — *What We Do For Love*
Fred Skolnik— *Americans and Other Stories*
Lynn Sloan — *This Far Is Not Far Enough*
L.E. Smith — *Views Cost Extra*
Caitlin Hamilton Summie — *To Lay To Rest Our Ghosts*
Susan Thomas — *Among Angelic Orders*
Tom Walker — *Signed Confessions*
Silas Dent Zobal — *The Inconvenience of the Wings*

Odd Birds
William Benton — *Eye Contact: Writing on Art*
Micheal Breiner — *the way none of this happened*
J. C. Ellefson — *Under the Influence: Shouting Out to Walt*
David Ross Gunn — *Cautionary Chronicles*
Andrei Guriuanu and Teknari — *The Darkest City*
Gail Holst-Warhaft — *The Fall of Athens*
Roger Lebovitz — *A Guide to the Western Slopes and the Outlying Area*
Roger Lebovitz — *Twenty-two Instructions for Near Survival*
dug Nap— *Artsy Fartsy*
Delia Bell Robinson — *A Shirtwaist Story*
Peter Schumann — *Belligerent & Not So Belligerent Slogans from the
                    Possibilitarian Arsenal*
Peter Schumann — *Bread & Sentences*
Peter Schumann — *Charlotte Salomon*

Fomite

Peter Schumann — *Diagonal Man, Volumes One and Two*
Peter Schumann — *Faust 3*
Peter Schumann — *Planet Kasper, Volumes One and Two*
Peter Schumann — *We*

Plays
Stephen Goldberg — *Screwed and Other Plays*
Michele Markarian — *Unborn Children of America*

Essays
Robert Sommer — *Losing Francis: Essays on the Wars at Home*